THE TEMPEST TALES

BOOKS BY WALTER MOSLEY
PUBLISHED BY WASHINGTON SQUARE PRESS

Devil in a Blue Dress
A Red Death
White Butterfly
Black Betty
A Little Yellow Dog
Gone Fishin'
Six Easy Pieces
Always Outnumbered, Always Outgunned
RL's Dream

WALTER MOSLEY

THE TEMPEST TALES
A NOVEL-IN-STORIES

W

WASHINGTON SQUARE PRESS

New York London Toronto Sydney

Washington Square Press
A Division of Simon & Schuster, Inc.
1230 Avenue of the Americas
New York, NY 10020

Originally published in hardcover in 2008 by Black Classic Press
Published by arrangement with Black Classic Press, Inc.

Alternate versions of portions of this work appeared in *Savoy* magazine in 2001.

First Washington Square Press trade paperback edition June 2009

WASHINGTON SQUARE PRESS and colophon are registered trademarks of Simon & Schuster, Inc.

For information about special discounts for bulk purchases, please contact Simon & Schuster Special Sales at 1-866-506-1949 or business@simonandschuster.com.

The Simon & Schuster Speakers Bureau can bring authors to your live event. For more information or to book an event contact the Simon & Schuster Speakers Bureau at 1-866-248-3049 or visit our website at www.simonspeakers.com.

Manufactured in the United States of America

10 9 8 7 6 5 4 3 2 1

Library of Congress Cataloging-in-Publication Data

Mosley, Walter
The tempest tales / Walter Mosley.—1st Washington Square Press trade pbk. ed.
    p. cm.
1. African American men—Fiction. 2. Wrongful death—Fiction. 3. Future life—Fiction. 4. Supernatural—Fiction. 5. Good and evil—Fiction. 6. Angels—Fiction. 7. Harlem (New York, N.Y.)—Fiction. I. Title.
PS3563.O88456T46 2009
813'.54—dc22   2008043061

ISBN 978-1-4165-9949-4

DEDICATED TO THE MEMORY OF
LANGSTON HUGHES

THE FALL

LIFE AND DEATH

TEMPEST LANDRY DIDN'T see himself as a bad man. He had a wife, whom he loved, a steady girlfriend, who loved him passionately, and various women on the side. All in all he had fourteen children, which was impressive because he was only thirty-four years old when he died.

Not a thief by nature, he would pick up a dollar tip if it was lying on a table and no one was looking. If there was a key in a door he'd turn the lock to see what was on the other side. If a man was selling anything from steak knives to steaks on the corner he wouldn't ask for a vendor's license if the street sales-man didn't charge tax.

Tempest loafed when he could and worked when he had to. He remembered his wife's anniversary and the birthdays of all his children and girlfriends. And though he had been arrested on various occasions he had never been convicted of a felony nor had he spent more than a week in jail.

Tempest wasn't ashamed of his history, but neither was he the victim of pride. He had been in seven serious fights since the age of fourteen and though some blood had been shed no one had died. He was always courteous with policemen, and so in the last few seconds of life he was miffed that they could shoot him down the way they did when he had never so much as used the "f" word when they rousted him in the street or from out of his own bed.

In a way it was technology that killed him and not the police at all. His steady girl, Alfreda, had bought him a mini disc player that didn't work right. It would get half the way through a tune and then switch channels or tracks or something so that suddenly it would be playing a whole other song. Tempest was walking up Adam Clayton Powell in Harlem, headed home to show his wife the new toy. Little did he know that an armed robber, Frank Elsworthy, had just robbed the new Starbucks coffee shop on 125th.

Tempest was wearing tan slacks and a dark, square-cut shirt, and so was Frank. They were both Negro and under forty. The thief was armed and desperate; Tempest had a mini disc player in his pocket that wouldn't play right, which made him mad.

And so when Frank cut east on 127th the police missed it and set their sights on Tempest. There were sirens but Lauryn Hill drowned them out. In the middle of "Killing Me Softly" the music went dead. Tempest shoved his hand in his pocket and pulled out the mini disc player, ready to throw it on the pavement. All of a sudden he got the twitching fits. Something was hitting him and then he was on the ground, tasting blood.

Lauryn Hill began singing again as Tempest faded from life.

THE NEXT THING TEMPEST knew, he was standing in a long line of people that ran down from a steep mountain trail. To his left there was a hazy landscape where furtive figures moved back and forth deep inside the gloomy fog. To the right was a vast plain of rolling hills and valleys under a bright sky with clouds that made him think of God.

Though there were people before and behind Tempest, many thousands of them, for some reason he couldn't focus on anyone's face. Miles up ahead a large man sat at a granite table, hunched over a large book that Tempest knew instinctively was a volume in the great compilation of the sins of man.

It seemed odd to Tempest that he could see the old man and his book so clearly when they were many miles away, but he still could not make out the face of the man, or woman, behind him.

St. Peter looked up at a sad soul before him and read a long list of complaints that we accounting angels had compiled during the man's life. There were thefts and lies, an abused child, and some sort of insurance fraud that Tempest didn't quite understand.

The man, whoever he was, had stolen a jar of cash out of his dead mother's home before his brother arrived from St. Louis for the funeral. The list was long but the judge read it patiently, without anger or acrimony.

The man, for his part, nodded every time a complaint was read, saying, "I know, I know," the saddest defeat in his voice.

Finally Peter looked up with blue-gray eyes that had deep furrows at their corners. He seemed so sorrowful that Tempest felt near tears. Peter uttered a word and with only a gasp the sinner turned to his left and wandered off into the foggy limbo that Tempest now understood must be the outer edge of hell.

It was then that Tempest realized that each one of the ever growing line of dead souls had witnessed this judgment. This was death, and every man, woman, and child who died were onlookers to eternity.

Tempest had never been a patient man. His mother said

that instead of crying he thanked the doctor for his liberation. "He was crawlin' by two months," Mrs. Landry used to say. "He was runnin' before he could walk."

It was true that Tempest never sat still.

"Maybe if they taught history on the basketball court," he told his teacher, "I might get somethin', but you know it's hell sittin' in this chair."

Tempest was impatient, fretful, and always on the verge of getting angry, but not on that final line. He approached his maker's judge with the same deep interest he had for Oprah and Doctor Phil. Several times he tried to engage his neighbors in conversation about the nature of some sins. Like the woman who had murdered her sister for using her own perfume while committing adultery with her husband.

"That there's a hard one," Tempest said to the soul in front of him. "I guess the woman borrowed the perfume to save her sister the pain of smelling another woman's scent on her man. Do you think they both got sent to the left?"

The soul ahead did not answer. Tempest wondered if he even heard him. Maybe everybody was chattering away, Tempest thought, but the rule of heaven had made them mute.

After many thousands of judgments; after millions of sins, from blasphemy to murder, Tempest found himself standing before St. Peter.

"Tempest Landry," the judge spoke.

"Here," Tempest said.

The old man might have smiled before turning the page of his great book.

"You stabbed Quentin Sams on July sixteenth when you were only fifteen."

"Excuse me, your honor, but that there was in self-defense.

Q-boy was reachin' for the pistol in his pocket when he saw me kissin' on a girl who had broke it off with him that mornin'."

Peter looked up from his book with pique in his visage. No one had seen such a look since the Mahatma had refused the refuge of heaven.

Running a finger down the page Peter again began reading, "At eighteen you stole three hundred and fourteen dollars from your mother's own church."

"Actually," Tempest said, holding up his hands as if to apologize for his impudence, "I know it looks like I stole from the church but really I only took from Reverend Langly. I mean I had seen him down at Bertha Burnett's cat house throwin' away the congregation's money on the women and liquor. And I used that money to pay for my auntie's groceries while she was out of work and recoverin' from the pneumonia. The way I saw it I was takin' the church's money away from the devil and puttin' it to work for God the way it was meant to be used."

Peter's stare this time lasted more than the three months needed to separate sin from saintliness in the arrogant Joan of Arc.

When Peter went back to his notes there was no compassion left in his voice.

"You bore false witness against Tiny Henderson when you knew that he was innocent. Your lies," all of us on duty that day were sure that the word lies was not in the record, "helped to convict this man of a brutal crime which he did not commit."

"Now, judge, I admit that there's some gray area in these other accusations but in the case of Henderson versus Harlem-in-general I think that you would have to agree that it was my duty to bear false witness against that neighbor."

"What do you mean?" St. Peter asked.

This was unthinkable. No guardian of heaven's gate had

ever questioned a soul before him. Never. The choir began murmuring. The line of millions of souls heard our consternation as beautiful music.

"I mean," Tempest replied to the keeper's question, "that Tiny Henderson had brutalized, raped, and murdered throughout our community and had not been convicted or jailed for years. I knew a man that he killed. I heard him brag on it. So when I lied before that magistrate it was really a truth, just that he hadn't done one thing but he had done another."

Peter slammed the book shut and pointed angrily toward the foggy limbo that led unerringly to eternal damnation.

"Go to hell!" the saint commanded.

"No," Tempest said.

The choir went silent.

"No?"

"You said what I did and I gave you my reasons why. But you didn't come back and explain why my whys were wrong."

Another month of celestial time passed as Peter studied the strange man before him.

"You honestly feel that you are virtuous?" Peter asked.

"I ain't no virgin," Tempest said. "But then again, I ain't no sinner neither."

"Then you will not follow my direction and enter into damnation?"

"Not unless you can prove to me I done wrong. Either that or throw me in the pit yourself."

Peter nodded and Tempest disappeared from the eternal procession of justice.

THREE YEARS AFTER HIS death Tempest reappeared on the corners of 135th and Lenox. He was wearing the same clothes but his body was changed. He was still a black man, still under forty but he had a new face that no one would have recognized as Tempest Landry.

I walked up to him then and said, "Hello, Tempest. Welcome back to earth."

"Who are you?"

"I am your angel. Either vengeful or guardian, that is up to you."

"Angel? You mean that wasn't no dream?"

"Look in the glass," I said.

He followed my suggestion and fell back in shock.

"What happened to me?"

"The Infinite has thrown you back, Tempest. And I have been sent along to monitor your progress."

"Progress in what?"

"You told the keeper that you saw no sin in your life."

"How do you know?"

"I was there. I was sent to help you reexamine the circumstances of that life. When you agree that the judgment against you was true then you will enter immediately into hell."

"And if I don't agree?"

"If not there will be a great turmoil in the heavens."

Tempest paused a moment to gauge the weight of my words.

"Are you a black man or are you just a white man made up to look like he was black?" he asked.

"I am an angel, like I said. Not black or white, not man at all."

"So you're not a white man then?"

"No."

"Okay then, as long as you could be fair I'll give it a go. You prove to me that I'm a sinner or I prove to you that there's more to me than you know."

And so began the story of Tempest Landry, three years after his death in Harlem, USA.

CHARITY

I WAS WAITING TO meet Tempest at Reno's Bar and Restaurant at six o'clock that Friday evening. We had agreed on the day of his resurrection that he would spend two weeks getting used to the world after his three years away in Celestial Court.

It was already eight thirty and I was tired because part of my job, as Tempest's attendant angel, was to assume a mortal identity. I had taken a position as an accountant at Rendell, Chin, and Mohammed on Fortieth Street near the library. I decided that since it had been my job from the dawn of humanity to keep an accounting of mortal sins that bookkeeping was probably my forte.

I was good at my job but mortality presented hitherto unforeseen problems. In the City of God time had no meaning. If I needed a moment or a hundred years to research a problem there was always enough time. But at the accounting firm I was continually under deadline, and most of the time I was late.

That morning I had gotten to the office at six and worked

straight through coffee breaks and lunch. I was late getting to Reno's, which is way up in Harlem, but not as late as Tempest.

I decided to give him five minutes more before I went to my small apartment on Staten Island. I was very tired, and even though the next day was Saturday they expected me to come in to work to catch up on my quarterly tax reports.

I was just standing up to leave when Tempest walked in the front door. He was wearing the same square-cut shirt and tan slacks but they were a little worse for wear.

"Where the hell have you been?" he asked as he stormed up to my table.

"Have a seat, Mr. Landry," I replied.

He pulled out a chair and fell into it like a petulant child angry at some injustice inflicted by his mother.

"So?" he asked. "Where have you been?"

"I don't understand. We agreed to meet today, didn't we?"

"We sure did. But I agreed to that before I looked in my pockets. When I was shot down by those cops I had a hundred and some dollars in my pocket. My girlfriend Alfreda had lent it to me to pay for my wife's medication. Glenda was sick and the antibiotic was eighty-nine sixty-five."

"And your girlfriend agreed to pay for your wife's medicine?"

"If she didn't I'da had to work overtime and then when would we get to see each other? But that's not the problem," Tempest complained. "The problem was that there wasn't no money whatsoever in my pocket when I was brought back here. I had my same clothes, my same socks and shoes. I had the same holes in my socks that I had when they killed me. So if the Infinite can gimme back my life, down to the holes in my socks, then why in the world would He wanna pick my pocket?"

"It's all part of the test," I said.

"What test? I don't remember agreein' to take no test."

"Your life on earth is meant to be a reexamination of your sins . . ."

"So-called sins," Tempest said, correcting me.

"What we in heaven call sins," I said.

"What I call tryin' t'live a life when the people who say they care about you don't really give a damn."

"What did you do when you found you had no money?"

"You mean, how did I survive after you picked my pockets clean?"

I smiled and indicated to the bartender that I wanted another glass of red wine. Wine is just about the only accepted vice in heaven. That and pipe smoking.

"First thing I did was to look for you. Well no, the first thing I did was go to the store to buy me some aspirin because you left me with the aches of them bullets that cut me down."

"It's a trick of the mind, the soul," I said. "Your body is a new one but your mind is still close to that accidental shooting."

"Now there you go again," Tempest said, pointing at me with the fingers of both hands. "You say stuff just like your boss, stuff like somethin' is true when it ain't. Them shootin' me wasn't no accident. You don't take no scared white boys can't tell the difference between one black man and another, give 'em guns, and let 'em run around the streets of Harlem and then say it was an accident when they one day shoot down an innocent man. Was it an accident that time they arrested me and beat me and tried to get me to confess to a crime I didn't commit? No, no. I don't think them cops killed me did it outta spite but it sure wasn't no accident neither. The accident was me bein' a black man out in the open."

"I only meant to say," I said, "that your mind remembered the pain of your death. That's why you needed the painkiller."

"Only when I got up to the register and reached for the money Alfreda give me I found out that I was broke."

"And what did you do then?"

"What do you think? I put the medicine back on the shelf and walked out of the store with the security guard watchin' to make sure that the alarm don't go off when I passed through the security system. Security system," Tempest said with disgust. "They got us livin' like we was in prison and then get mad when we steal."

"Did you find a job?" I asked. "I mean, an honest man, when he finds himself broke, looks for employment to fill his pockets."

Mr. Tempest Landry looked at me then with deep suspicion.

"Are you sure that you ain't a white man under that black face, brother?"

"I told you already, I'm an angel not a mortal man. Race means no more to me than it does to the stars."

"I guess so," Tempest said. "Because in this day and age even a white man knows that you can't get a job without a phone number and that you can't get a phone number without a place to have a phone. Even a cell phone company need an address where they could send the bill at."

"I never considered that," I said. "It's true that when I applied for my job that I already had a place to receive mail."

"You got a job?" Tempest asked with real surprise in his voice.

"Well, of course. I have to survive as a mortal while we continue inquiry into your sins—"

"So-called sins."

"So-called sins," I agreed.

"So you got a job and apartment just like anybody else?"

"Why are you surprised? How else would I survive?"

"I never thought about it," Tempest said, seeming a little less angry. "I guess I figured that you went back up into heaven at night after checking on us restless souls."

"You are my only charge, Mr. Landry. You are the only soul in all the centuries of Peter's reign to challenge his judgment. Kings and popes have bowed down before his decrees with little less than a whimper. But you—"

"How much money they give you?" Tempest asked, cutting me off.

"I don't know," I said. "A hundred dollars."

"So they took my money and give it to you in order for you to keep an eye out for when I slip up and have to do what your boss say and go to hell."

"That's not what happened. You're the one that's being tested. I'm not on trial."

"But what's that got to do with my money?"

"Nothing," I said, confused by Tempest's angry claim.

"But you're an angel, right?"

"Yes."

"And angels don't have money up in heaven?"

"We don't need money."

"But we come down here and you get a hundred dollars while I get a hundred taken away. And now that I think of it you had to have more'n a hundred dollars 'cause the rent, even on the poorest crib, is more'n that."

"Go on," I said. I saw no reason to tell him that I also found a credit card and a checkbook in my wallet.

"All I'm tryin' to say is how can you judge me when you got it so easy that you cain't know how I feel?"

"I am not a judge," I said. "I am merely here to talk to you, to counsel you until you understand that you are not deserving of the kingdom of heaven."

"But how can you understand me if you can't understand what it feels like to be broke, homeless, and unknown even to your own mother?"

"I have aeons of experience with human suffering, Mr. Landry. I saw Moses rise up against the pharaohs, Attila the Hun rage across Europe. I've been in the gas chambers of Treblinka and I've witnessed African women sink in the cold Atlantic with their babies in their arms." I had raised my voice to express the drama of these experiences and found that there were people around the bar area staring at me.

"But," Tempest asked pointedly, "have you ever been hungry?"

"Excuse me?"

"Have you ever bled, hurt, or went without?"

I wanted to speak but there were no words to say.

"Have you ever even lost a friend?" Tempest asked.

I hunched my shoulders. I had never lost anything. No angel ever had.

"So you see when I tell you that I was hungry or achin' I don't think that you could understand. I went to my mother's house and she answered the door and looked at me with the same suspicious look that she has for bill collectors. How would you know how it felt? You couldn't. You never could."

"We aren't here to question my understanding. It is you who has to understand."

"And I think it's you," Tempest said. "Bartender! Give me a sour mash double shot and put it on his tab."

"I have to go soon," I said when the drinks came. I put a twenty-dollar bill down on the table. "I'm tired."

"Angels get tired?"

"I've been working hard. And as long as I'm here I am as mortal as you."

"I doubt that."

"Would you like to have money for the rent, Mr. Landry?" I realized that he was right, that I should at least let him get his feet on the ground before trying to convince him that he is a sinner.

"No. I got a place."

"How did you manage that with no job?"

"I lifted a United Charities Fund contribution box that they got in Hildebrandt's department store. Then I took the forty-seven bucks I got from there and paid it to a guy I knew when I was alive, a guy who supplies street vendors with fancy watch knockoffs to sell to the rubes that think there's somethin' for nuthin' somewhere in the world."

"You stole?"

"Not from the way I look at it. That contribution box is for charity, charity is for the poor, and I was just about as poor as you can get. I figured that the money, if it got collected, would have to go through about a dozen hands before it got to some-body like me. That forty-seven twenty-nine I got prob'ly wouldn't be no more than twenty bucks by then. I just cut out the middleman and went into business on my own."

"But you stole—"

"And that was wrong. But I give the money back and I used it for what it was meant for. Now I got a place and I'm startin' a real job at a restaurant downtown."

"You admit that you were wrong?"

"Not so wrong that I deserve hell."

I wanted to argue but I was too tired.

"Let's get together in the reading room of the public library on Forty-second Street on Sunday afternoon," I suggested. "We can talk about it more then."

Tempest and I left together. He walked me to the subway and shook my hand at the stairs.

"See you Sunday, Angel," he said.

His attitude surprised me. There was no more ire or condemnation. He'd expressed his anger and let it go.

I dozed all the way to South Ferry, wondering who was being tested after all.

THE KINGDOM OF HEAVEN

WHEN I ARRIVED at the library that Sunday at noon I found Tempest already there paging through a dictionary. He saw me and frowned. Then he made a gesture of resignation with his shoulders and nodded at the chair next to his.

I sat and said hello.

"So how's this supposed to work?" he asked.

"What?"

"You know," he said peevishly. "How are you supposed to trip me up so that I have to go to hell?"

"I'm not here to trick you."

"No? Then tell me, do you think that I'm such a bad sinner that I deserve eternal damnation?"

"That was Peter's decree."

"I ain't askin' him."

"It is the judgment of heaven that you have used your free will in vain, that you are, are . . ."

"Are what?"

"Shhh," a young woman with red dreadlocks hissed from two tables away.

"Let's go outside where we won't be bothering anyone with our talk," I suggested.

Tempest shrugged and stood up.

Together we walked down the stairs to the Forty-second Street exit and passed through the security checkpoint. The guard there stopped me because I passed her without a word or gesture.

"Excuse me, sir! Excuse me," the woman said.

"Yes?"

"I have to look in your briefcase."

"Why?" I asked.

"Because that's the rules," the woman insisted.

I opened my case, which held various files from the accounting firm of Rendell, Chin, and Mohammed. They had over four hundred tax returns for me to process. And since Tempest was almost three hours late to our last meeting, I'd decided to bring some work along so as not to waste time. Time, that most precious and strange aspect of mortal existence.

The guard went through the pages.

"Are you through?" I asked.

"Listen, mister," she replied. "I'm just doin' my job. There's no reason for you to get rude with me."

I closed my case and went outside to meet Tempest.

He led me around to the Fifth Avenue entrance. There we sat on the great staircase.

"So?" Tempest asked again. "How does it work?"

"You have been allowed a chance to prove your claim that you are not a sinner and that you should be welcome in the kingdom of heaven."

"And how can I do that?"

"By proving virtue."

"Is that my own virtue or the goodness in others?"

"Whatever you want to talk about. We will meet and discuss and decide between ourselves if your life has been on the path to righteousness or no. You see heaven, for all races and religions, is based on free will. It is your personal belief in the Infinite which saves or condemns."

"So I can't go to hell except if I agree that I did wrong?"

"Exactly."

"That don't sound right to me," Tempest said.

"What about it don't you understand?" I asked, wishing to help my mortal charge.

"I understand all of it. It just stinks, that's all."

"You aren't making any sense, Mr. Landry."

"I must be makin' some kinda sense, Angel. I must be makin' some kinda sense, otherwise you'd be back up in the choir and I'd be cookin' on Satan's spit."

"This kind of talk, this human relativism, will get us nowhere."

"I don't know what that 'r' word means but I understand nowhere. Nowhere was where I was when I was waitin' in line for St. Peter to blame me for the trouble that was my life before the police murdered me."

"You were not murdered," I said, trying to sound reasonable. Tempest had irritated even the eternally sanguine Peter. "The men who killed you did not have murder in their hearts."

"Did they kill me?"

"Yes, but—"

"Did I do anything that they should kill me for?"

"No, however—"

"Did they mean to kill me?"

"Not specifically, but they knew that there was a, a—"

"One man means to kill another man, an unarmed man,

and then he kills him; that's murder in my book—especially when you add in there that the man gettin' killed is innocent."

"You were making some other point, I believe," I said.

"Yeah, yeah." Tempest seemed to have lost the thread of his argument. The look on his face was more one of confusion than anything else.

"Would you like me to remind you of what we were saying? As an accounting angel, I remember everything."

"Rememberin' somethin' an' knowin' it is two different things."

"What do you mean?" I asked.

"You look like a black man but you're not, right?"

"No, I am—"

"I know what you are," he said. "I know what you say. Like you said that I decide, not Peter."

"That's true."

"Then why ain't I up in heaven with you right now?"

"Because there's a difference of opinion about the state of your soul."

"Okay," Tempest said, making a generous gesture with his hands. "So it's up to somebody else."

"Whether or not you ascend to the kingdom is up to us, but the entrance to damnation must be your own choice."

"So that's the first lie," Tempest said. "It's not up to me but to you. The second problem is this racism that you puttin' on me."

"Racism!" I cried. "Now this is too much. There is no race in heaven."

"We ain't in heaven, brother. This is New York City. This is where I washed up through no fault of my own. Down here the color of your skin means somethin'. And this sin you say is on me happened here, or just a few miles north up there in Harlem."

"So you're telling me that you are innocent because you were born to a world that tested your virtue?"

"I ain't said nuthin' 'bout bein' no innocent," Tempest shouted. Here and there on the white marble stairs heads turned to see what the problem was. "Do only people who never sinned go to heaven?"

"Of course not."

"Well then, how much sin is too much?"

"That is decided on a person-by-person basis."

"So if a man only commits one sin but he did five things good, then maybe he gets up to heaven."

"Maybe."

"But if a man do twenty things good but commits twenty-one sins, then he goes to hell."

"I don't know, Tempest. There are no hard-and-fast rules."

"Them bullets struck me down was hard-and-fast enough. They hurt too."

"What is your point?"

"You tell me I got free will only if I try an' use it you say the choice ain't up to me. You tell me that I can prove my innocence but then say that there ain't rules to say what's right and what's wrong. You show me the face of a black man and then say that there ain't no race. And finally you try'n fool me with this kingdom of heaven stuff."

"Fool you?"

"Yes, fool me. My kingdom is Lenox and 135. I don't want your Elysian Fields or pearly gates or wings. I'll take some chicken wings. I'll take Alfreda's pearly smile. And the football field be good enough for me. I never asked you to judge me . . ."

Suddenly I was struck with mortal dread. For all eternity I had existed above the temporal realm secure in the omnipotence of my beliefs. But as Tempest spoke a coldness passed through the core of my being. I realized that he was a moment away from dismissing his belief in me; that this rejection could well end my existence. A few words from this ordinary man and I, who was immortal up until that moment, would pass forever from the world.

I awaited his decree as helpless as the untold billions who had stood before the various judges of heaven's gate and their book.

". . . I never asked you to judge me," Tempest was saying, "but bring it on. I ain't afraid'a you. You think you could prove me wrong but it's you who's wrong. You, not me."

"I see," I said. Inside I was rejoicing. Everything I believed in was saved by Tempest's stubborn rage.

When I said no more he wrote down his phone number and told me to call when I wanted to talk more.

"Next time," he said. "Come on uptown. That's where the puddin' is."

"The pudding?" I asked, still weak from my first bout of mortal fear.

"That's where the proof is," Tempest said with a smile and a wink.

DESIRE

IT HAD BEEN nearly a month since I'd seen Tempest. The last time we had met, on the steps of the New York Public Library on Forty-second and Fifth, I had a rather bad shock.

However, I realized at our last meeting that Tempest had the power to refute the claims of heaven. I was struck with the mortal dread that if Tempest rejected the Infinite the heaven I knew would cease to exist. So for four weeks I had considered how to approach my charge and his convoluted notions of right and wrong.

I finally called him from work on a Wednesday morning at eleven thirty-nine. I had just finished preparing the last of four hundred and sixteen quarterly tax returns for my bosses at the accounting firm of Rendell, Chin, and Mohammed. They liked my work but had complained that I was too slow. Me—the accounting angel of St. Peter—too slow in the estimation of mere mortal bookkeepers.

Tempest agreed to meet with me at a bar called Lucifer's Lair. I suppose he meant that as some kind of comment on our relationship, but I went with the conviction of my beliefs and certainty of my goals.

"Hey, Angel," Tempest said as I climbed into the seat across from him in one of the two booths of the storefront bar.

"Mr. Landry," I said in greeting.

He had a glass of red wine waiting for me.

"How's the job?" Tempest asked.

"I caught up with all my work. They were going to fire me but I put in some extra hours and now all they do is sing my praises."

"Must make you feel right at home," Tempest replied.

I noted a sour tone in his voice and so asked, "Is anything wrong?"

"Is anything right? That's what you should ask me."

"What's the problem?"

"Glenda and the kids, that's what." Tempest lit a cigarette, drew in, then blew out a great gust of smoke. "The kids don't know who I am and Glenda got a new man."

"It's been three years since you died, Tempest—"

"But I ain't dead," he said. "I'm flesh and bone, needs and desires just like any other man. I love my kids and now they callin' Rix Mulgrew Daddy."

"Children need a father," I said.

"Well here I am, ain't I? I'm their daddy but they don't even know me. I took an apartment in the same building on 147th. I tried to talk to the kids a couple'a times but they just run away from me. My own kids. That's when Rix Mulgrew come down an' tell me that him and Glenda wanted me to leave Nina and Bobby alone or that they were gonna call the police—on me! Here I am all alone, dead to the world but still breathin'. Nobody knows me. Nobody see me says hi, Tempest." Tempest shook his head sadly and gestured to the waitress for another drink.

"Then why do you insist on staying?" I asked, seizing upon the opportunity. "There's a place waiting for you."

Tempest looked at me hopelessly. For a moment I thought he would accept the judgment of heaven.

"No," he said instead. "I didn't do anything to deserve this. Why should I pay for them cops shootin' me down and Peter refusin' me heaven? Why should I pay the price just 'cause Glenda don't recognize me and Alfreda do me like she do?"

"Alfreda? What about her?" Alfreda was Tempest's girl-friend while he was married to Glenda. That was one mark against his bid for eternal bliss.

"When Glenda didn't know me I went down to Alfreda's place to see if she might see somethin' of the old me in this new body's eyes. She had moved but the old man across the hall knew where she had gone to. So I went over there and knocked on her door."

"And did she know you?"

"No. But I had a story for her. I said that I had seen her when she worked at the beauty shop on 125th Street when I used to get my groceries at the store next door. I said that I had wanted to meet her but then I took ill and I had to go down South for a while. Now, I knew that she was from the South and so we had a few words to share there. I told her that I went back to the beauty shop to find her but she was gone, that they gave me her address but she had moved but the old man across the hall pointed me in the right direction.

"One thing led to another and we had dinner together. Dinner led to a walk home and the next thing you know we was gettin' comfortable."

"That doesn't sound lonely to me," I said. I was feeling a lit-tle guilty for trying to prey on Tempest's moment of weakness.

"You'd think so, now wouldn't you?"

"What was wrong?"

"Well, I knew Alfreda pretty good. You know . . . I know what she likes. We were havin' a pretty good time there and she was happy, very happy with me."

"All that sounds like something to make you glad."

"It was. It was. Up until she told me that I was the best lover she had ever known."

"What could be wrong with that?"

"What about me? Not me here but the old me—Tempest Landry before he died? At first I didn't let it bother me too much. But as the night wore on it started to get to me. Finally I just had to ask her how she could tell a man after only half an evening that he was the best she ever knew? What about the men she had known in her past? Men who had bought her flowers and studied her moods, men who had sat with her while she was sick or sad?"

"And what did she say then?"

"She stood by her guns, said that I was the best man who ever shared her bed. And the more she said it the angrier I got. Finally I grabbed my clothes and lit outta there. She was hangin' on my arm beggin' me t'stay but I just couldn't. I felt as if I was betrayin' myself makin' that woman call out to me while forgettin' who I was."

"So you were jealous of yourself?" I asked. There was a grin on my face, which might not be unusual for men, but for angels smiles are as rare as saints are among men.

"Yes, I was," Tempest said. "How could she tell a man she hadn't known but a few hours that he was the love of her life? My name never even came up as a close second."

"Maybe she loved you so much because she missed you," I suggested. "Maybe it was her unconscious mind that knew you and loved you."

"It was her conscious mouth callin' out the name I made up when I made my pass at her. 'Albert!' she cried in my arms. 'Oh Lord yes, Albert!' I swear it was just like standin' outside the door hearin' your woman with another man. Made me so mad that I left her in between kisses."

"I guess that must feel terrible," I said, trying to show some empathy for my mortal charge.

"You guess? Don't you know how it feels?"

"Not really. Angels don't have those kinds of relationships. To begin with we're all male, though not in a sexual way, and there is no congress, no particular relationship among us."

"There ain't no women up in heaven?"

"Mortal souls, yes. But the angels, like I said, are all one sexless gender."

"So you don't have girlfriends or boyfriends or whatever? There's just you. No baby angels. No marriage."

"No."

"Then how can you judge me on adultery or jealousy or covetin' what I ain't got but I want in the worst way?"

"One does not have to commit a murder to judge a murderer," I said.

"But you got to know passion and rage. You got to know when a man get pushed so far that he acts from his heart and not from sin."

"We have studied passion," I said, rather lamely.

"You gonna have to feel passion if you want me to say whether or not I agree with your verdict on my butt."

"What do you mean by that?"

"I mean . . ." Tempest paused, struggling with his anger at Glenda, Alfreda, and heaven. After a few seconds he continued, "I was on the street one day down around the Port Authority. This was a long time ago, long before I died. There was this poor woman with three babies sittin' outside beggin' for money. Her oldest child wasn't even five and the youngest was still in diapers. The woman was pitiful, holdin' out her hands for anything that someone might give. I was just a part of the crowd walkin' by. For some reason I didn't give her anything, I just didn't but there was no reason. I was walkin' next to these well-dressed white ladies who started talkin' when they were out from the poor woman's earshot. 'She should get a job,' one woman said to the other. And the other said, 'The state should take her poor children too. It's a shame what she's making them go through.'

"Now, when I heard that I doubled back and gave the woman one of my two five-dollar bills. Who did those white ladies think they were, passin' judgment like that? I mean, how's a woman with three babies gonna get a job? And what good is the state gonna do by takin' them children when ain't nobody ever gonna love 'em like that mother do?

"You're like them white ladies. Pass judgment on my heart when you don't know a thing."

"I agree with you, Mr. Landry," I said.

"Say what?"

"I agree with you. I never knew what work was like until I became mortal and experienced the pressure of time passing. But you will have to help me, to show me what you think I should do to feel what you feel. Because you see I still believe in the judgment of heaven. And I will not shirk from any method I need to employ to prove to you that you are a sinner."

"You agree to experience pain and jealousy and hunger too?"

"I do."

"Well damn. If you willin' to do that, then I agree to play

fair with you. If you can show me how I could'a lived better, then I will accept your will, or Peter's at least."

"Then we have a deal," I said.

"We have a deal," Tempest echoed.

We shook hands and I laughed out loud for the first time that I could ever remember.

TRINITY

THE NEXT TIME I met Tempest he was at an outside picnic table facing the East River at the back side of the South Street Seaport in downtown Manhattan. He had left word for me at my office that we should meet there for lunch on Wednesday afternoon. This presented a problem with my employers—Rendell, Chin, and Mohammed, the tax accountants. My lunch break was only an hour and it would take much longer than that to get down to the seaport tourist attraction, have our meeting, and then return. But I agreed because it was my prime function to make the deceased and resurrected Harlemite realize his life of sin and accept Peter's judgment of eternal damnation.

So I left my earthly job at eleven fifteen to make sure I met Tempest at the appointed picnic table. He was waiting for me but he wasn't alone. Seated next to him was another aged black man.

I was disturbed to see Tempest and the older black man sitting there talking and drinking beer. The business of heaven, I thought, was not a matter for public display. We were fighting over the future of immortality—every soul that ever lived, that ever would live, hung in the balance of our debates.

"Hey, Angel," Tempest called when he saw me. His friend turned to regard me but there didn't seem to be any awe or suspicion in his eye. "I brought you some red wine," Tempest continued, holding up a brown bag that was obviously wrapped over a wine bottle, "and a chili cheese dog with fries and catsup."

I came up to the table, staring at Tempest and ignoring his friend.

"This is LaVon," Tempest said, gesturing toward the man I pretended was not there. "I told him that you'n me get together to talk about right and wrong and stuff like that. He said that that was his specialty and so I said why don't he come along."

"I thought our talks were supposed to be private," I said, the icy expanse of heaven in my tone.

"Nobody ever said anything about that to me," Tempest responded. He was smiling this day, not sad as at our last meeting.

"I thought it was obvious," I replied.

"You mean obvious like sin is to good men?"

His question caught me off guard. Up until that moment I thought that Tempest was an unintelligent man who's stubborn nature was all that heaven had to fear. But I saw then that he was clever, even calculating. A man of such intelligence was a greater threat than I had feared.

"It doesn't matter," I said, sliding into the seat next to the man named LaVon.

"Okay then," Tempest said. He slapped his hands together and then rubbed them like a hungry fly. "What should we talk about today?"

"Maybe Mr. . . ." I paused, hoping that our elder guest would offer his last name.

"Just call me LaVon," he said instead. "That's what every-one do."

"Well, LaVon," I said, determined not to be thrown off course by Tempest's tricks. "What do you know about sin?"

LaVon was maybe sixty but he wasn't holding up very well. The whites of his eyes were tending toward brown and his breath had the stench of disease. His cheeks were sunken and his hair was sporadic, appearing in some places and gone in others. Even his white facial hairs seemed to be stalling, almost too strained to grow. He wore a threadbare and faded pink T-shirt that had MANATEES CARIBBEAN HAVEN written across the chest.

"Sin is the bane of man," the elder LaVon said in a surpris-ingly deep and musical voice. "It is what turns us every day from the Garden of Eden and it is the test of every man. The harder the test the greater the virtue. But you know I'd rather get a average 'C' than have to suffer the trials of Job or Abraham."

I was surprised by the eloquence and deep feelings of LaVon's words. I was expecting something else from a man of his appearance; anger or bawdy humor, not words that I might have heard on the higher plane.

Out of the corner of my eye I noticed Tempest grinning at me.

"But you agree," I said, "that each man has his own test. One man can't look at another man's life and say, 'Look at how much easier so-and-so had it. You can't judge me by the same golden rule.'"

LaVon was a man near death, I could see that in his eyes. He squinted because of the daylight even though his back was toward the sun.

"No, you can't," he said, nodding in agreement with my words.

I couldn't help but turn toward Tempest and give him a smug grin.

". . . but," LaVon continued, "even though one man cannot compare himself to another in the eyes of the Lord he might take a moment to wonder why one whole race of people is made to suffer so much more than some others."

"I can't agree with that," I said, waving my hand to dismiss the man who seemed to be dying before my very eyes.

"Why not?" Tempest demanded.

"You have tried to call Peter and the rest (I refrained from adding 'of us') racists before, but that's ridiculous," I said with great pride. "There is no black and white in heaven. All souls are bodiless and colorless. No matter your religion or appreciation of the Infinite you are judged on the merit of your life."

"But what about the Jews?" LaVon asked. "They were thrown in the desert, drowned in the flood. As a people they were chosen but the choice wasn't one I'da begged for."

"The Bible," I said, picking the words slowly, "is a story. Any group of people referred to are just a metaphor for Man."

"Oh," LaVon said. He nodded but his neck muscles were so weak that his chin dipped lower and lower toward the table. "Then why is almost every picture I ever seen of Christ the picture of a white man? Is that some kinda poetry too?"

"That is an error," I said.

"Is error sin?" LaVon asked back.

I thought for a moment about this question. It was so deep a query that I forgot that I was in the mortal realm. In Infinity one has as long as he wishes to ponder and respond. A thousand years would not be too long to take before replying to some complex problem. I don't know how many minutes I thought but it was too long for an earthly reply.

"'Cause you see," LaVon said, "Christianity has excluded

black folks, Chinese, and Jews from the pantheon. We not angels or saints, pharaohs or kings—just people on the outside lookin' in. Is it an error to keep us out like that, or a sin? And is it right to punish a whole people if it's one on one when you get up to heaven's gate? That's the questions I ask myself, Mr. Angel. That's why I took the train down with my friend Tempest here. He told me that you was wise to these problems. You know I'ma die soon and I'd surely like to think that there was an answer to what I cannot understand."

"The answer is in your heart, LaVon," I said with more certainty in my voice than my heart.

"Tell me somethin', LaVon," Tempest said.

"What?"

"What would you do if you were up in front of St. Peter and he told you that you were a sinner and your lot was hell?"

The old man's eyes watered. Tempest's question was a reality that he soon expected.

"What could I do?" he replied. "What could I say?"

"You could say to him what you just said to Angel here. You could say that you seen some numbers that just don't add up," Tempest suggested to LaVon while staring into my eyes.

"No," LaVon said. "No, I couldn't. Heaven would suck the words outta my throat, I know that much for sure."

"But don't you have free will, LaVon?" Tempest asked to taunt me further.

"On earth I do," the old man said. "But past here is His realm. All I can do is obey no matter how much it hurts."

"So, Angel," Tempest continued. "It looks like I'm not the only one who thinks that some things might not be right in the world."

"It is not the question but the acceptance of the divine that matters," I said.

"If you question the word you don't accept it," he replied. "Even if you're silent that don't mean you agree."

"What did you do in life?" I asked LaVon, who was now resting his head on folded hands.

He looked up and attempted a smile. "I preached here and there," he said. "On a street corner or a storefront. I started in prison. They had me in there for armed robbery, you know."

"Oh," I said. "I didn't know that."

"Yeah." LaVon smiled and dozed off into a light sleep.

"Why did you bring him here?"

"Because'a what you said," Tempest replied seriously.

"What did I say that could have possibly included this tortured soul?"

"You said that we was all on trial. You and me and all of mankind. I'm not the only sinner feel virtuous. Here you got the entire Book of Sins at your disposal. You represent Peter and all the celestial choir. You haven't forgot a thing in a hunnert thousand years and here I don't remember the name of my mother's sister's husband. You got what they call a wealth of information. And knowledge is money even where I come from. So I figure since it's not just me, but all the poor souls, that sometimes you might wanna hear from somebody else who thinks like me but is scared to say so."

"But we aren't discussing LaVon's soul," I said with some tenderness. "He will face his own last judgment."

"But wasn't he brought there by poverty, under a smilin' white Lord?" Tempest asked. "Doesn't that matter to you?"

"Of course it does, my friend. But his spirit chose its own path. His life was his decision. I can only hope that he worked hard enough at his ministry to earn forgiveness and forever more."

"You see, Angel," Tempest said with a sad grin. "That's

where you'n me don't yet agree. And I will try and convince you still. When I look at LaVon Singleton here, I see a hero should be proclaimed and exalted. Not somebody who might have done good enough, but a champion come home after winnin' the title."

We both looked down on the napping street minister then. His sleep was now dreamless because LaVon had died. I knew it at once because the soul had fled. It took Tempest a moment more to discern the death.

When he realized his friend's passing he jumped up and looked about him frantically.

"Don't worry," I said. "He's on the great line already, waiting for the moment that you shunned."

"I got to find a doctor," Tempest said.

"It's too late for that," I said, but the words meant nothing to him. He looked right through me and then ran inside the seaport building.

I followed him and watched as he ran to a security guard and explained that his friend was sick. He made many people run around feeling for the lost pulse, calling the emergency line. Finally an ambulance came and the paramedics tried to revive LaVon. When they failed they still took him away, hoping for magic in their emergency room.

Tempest went after the ambulance. As I watched him trying to hail down a taxi I realized for the first time the full strength and majesty of life.

THE FIGHT

TEMPEST HAD TAKEN an apartment in a large building on East 147th Street. It had been more than three months since we had last met. He wasn't calling me and he hadn't answered my calls, so I decided to rekindle our talks about sin by waiting outside his building.

It was a very lively block with kids playing and many people coming and going about the business of their day. Due to my role as the accounting angel of Souls I began to assess the sins being committed by those around me. Small infractions as a rule: lies, adulterous seductions, threats, and using the name of the Infinite in vain. There was sloth and laziness and one man selling watches that I suspected were stolen.

No one there had to worry. I was on leave from my duties for a while. My only responsibility was Tempest Landry.

I loitered around for well over an hour, from six minutes after four o'clock till five forty-two. Tempest finally came down the concrete stairs of the tenement building, limping and bandaged, with one half-closed purple eye.

"Tempest!" I called across the street.

My voice is rather forceful and turned more than one head. Even though I had not called out their names, bystanders heard something in my voice, something that brings all humans ecstasy or dread.

Only Tempest was unmoved. He looked up and grimaced. He turned away, took three lame steps, and then turned back to wait for me as I ran across the street.

"What do you want?" he said.

"We agreed to talk, don't you remember?"

"I kinda lost my desire to conversate with you when LaVon was dyin' and you didn't even lift a finger to help him."

"He was dead, Tempest."

"You don't know that till the doctor says so."

"I do," I said.

For a moment there was a reply on Tempest's lips but that died away. He bit his lower lip and folded his arms across his chest.

"What do you want?" he asked again.

"What happened to you?"

"I got in a fight."

"Did you hurt anybody?" I asked.

"I got busted up pretty bad, or didn't you notice?"

"Well . . . I . . . How are you?"

"My left foot is fractured. I got fourteen stitches over my eye and the doctor says I might could have a concussion. And, oh yeah, I busted the big knuckle of my right hand on that hard-headed fool."

Tempest began walking again, down toward the subway. I went after him. It wasn't hard to keep up, because of his pronounced limp. While we were waiting for the No. 1 train I continued with our old subject—sin.

"Why were you fighting?"

"There's only two reasons to fight," Tempest said in his sourest tone. "One is to hurt somebody and the other is to stop somebody from hurting you. In my case it was one and then it was the other."

"I don't understand you."

"There was this little brown suitcase layin' on a bus stop bench over on the east side . . ." Just at that moment the train came. Tempest paused in his explanation because of the engines.

The train stopped and the doors slid open. The car was crowded and so we had to stand. The train hadn't gone very far when a young man, a Negro, stood up from his seat and indicated that Tempest should sit.

"You look like you could use it more than me, brother," the young man said.

I stood in the space before Tempest, looking down on him and hoping to continue our talk. Next to him sat a large brown woman with a happy baby perched on her knee.

"You were saying about a suitcase?" I prompted.

"Yeah," Tempest said. "I picked the suckah up. No, no, that's not right. First I scoped it out. I seen it layin' there and I watched it. Nobody did nuthin' about it so I figured I'd pop it open, see what was inside."

"Yes? What happened then?"

"Some big ugly dude come outta nowhere shoutin' at me an' tellin' me that that was his bag and I better hand it over or else I was gonna catch it."

"And did you return his suitcase?"

"I did not."

"Why not?"

"First off, who says that it was his? Maybe he saw it sittin' there too. Maybe he was waitin' like me to see if somebody was with it. Now here I moved first and he was mad 'cause he was too slow."

"Yeah," the young man who had given up his seat said.

I noticed that a few people standing around were listening to Tempest's story.

"So," I said, "you didn't believe this man owned the suitcase?"

"I did not and I told him so. I said that if he wanted that bag back he was gonna have to tell me what was inside it. Exactly what was inside it, not just say that there was a shirt and some underwear in there."

"And did he?"

"He started talkin' 'bout my mother. I mean he said some low-down things. And you know since my mother, uh, ain't talkin' to me . . . I'm very sensitive about her," he continued. "I told him to watch hisself." Tempest made an unconscious gesture with his fist, which told me what happened next.

"Thing is," Tempest continued, "he was a tough dog. I think he must'a done boxin' somewhere along the way. I finally took a step back and went upside his head with the suitcase. It busted all to hell and while he was tryin' to catch somethin' that went flyin' I put him down with my knuckle."

"He was trying to save the contents of the bag?" I asked.

Tempest nodded.

"Then it probably was his bag."

"Oh, it was his bag all right. It was nuthin' but some old clothes and photographs, two or three pair'a shoes. I could see by how he wanted to keep them pictures safe that they meant somethin' to him."

"Then you were guilty of theft and violence against your fellow man," I said in a voice that made the happy baby cry.

The yowling of the child distracted me from my purpose. Why was that lovely child so distraught to hear the judgment of heaven?

"He is not," the young man who had given up his seat complained.

"What do you mean?" I asked the man whose hair was braided in rows from the front of his head down the back of his neck.

"He saw that suitcase. It wasn't no one's, not when it was layin' there alone. An' if that dude left it then he better expect to explain himself. And if he don't then he better be ready to fight."

"The fact remains," I said, "that Tempest here took something that was not his and then he used violence to keep it. That is theft."

My voice was losing authority even though I attempted to dominate the young man's will with the command of heaven. The baby had stopped her crying. She was looking at me in wonder.

"It ain't stealin' if you pick somethin' up, Mister," the baby's young mother said. "And fightin' ain't bad if it's just gettin' mad. Damn, sometimes you get so mad you do things break your heart."

When she had said this, she caressed the child's cheek with a gentle finger. The baby cooed and rubbed her neck against her own shoulder.

"What you do after the suitcase busted open?" the young man asked Tempest.

"First I jumped back to see if he was reaching for a knife or somethin' he had had in the bag," Landry said, as if that was an eminently reasonable response.

The young mother and the courteous man, even the child seemingly, nodded their agreement.

"What then?" the mother asked.

"When I saw that he was just tryin' to get his stuff out the gutter I helped him. I told him I was sorry and folded his shirts while he put up the photographs in a little yellow Kodak paper jacket. His mother had died and they kicked him out of her apartment the day after the funeral. That bag, them pictures, was all he had left. We shook hands, then he got on the bus and that was the last I'll ever see of him."

"That's not stealin'," the young man pronounced. "That was just a misunderstandin', a flare-up. Around Harlem you either flare up or die of heart disease. Yeah. That's what they say."

"Uh-huh," the young mother chimed.

"My stop next," Tempest said.

For a moment I didn't know what he meant. I was thinking about that baby and the voices that made up her world. The train slowed down, came to a stop.

"Excuse me. Excuse me," Tempest Landry said as he made it toward the sliding doors.

I followed him out onto the Forty-second Street landing.

"If I didn't know better I would have said that you set that up," I told Tempest as people thronged around us heading toward their destinations.

"What?" he said. "You think we're dumb cows just 'cause we line up like cattle when we die and face oblivion?"

"Why did they forgive you?" I asked the nemesis of heaven.

"'Cause I haven't done anything wrong."

He turned and shambled away through the crowd. He went maybe thirty feet. He stopped and turned to see that I had not moved. He smiled at me and waved.

I made up my mind to converse with him privately from then on.

That night I couldn't get to sleep because I was thinking about that man, woman, and child. They had bested me and were still blameless. It was a moment unique in celestial history that will go unrecorded except in my personal journal.

LADY

S HE WAS STANDING next to an empty bench by a palm tree in downtown Manhattan. It was February and three inches of dirty snow covered the ground outside. She was young and pretty, even beautiful by certain earthly standards, but still I would not have noticed her except for where she was standing. Tempest had left word on my answering machine that he wanted to meet at the west-most southern bench in the World Financial Center's Hall of Palms.

I went to the bench and sat down with my newspaper. I read the paper every day trying to understand the quirk of human nature that would create a man like Tempest Landry, the heretic; a man who could deny the rule of heaven and refuse, actually refuse, the edicts of St. Peter. At first I thought my mission, to get Tempest to admit to his sins and enter into hell as decreed, would be a simple one. After all, he was only a mortal man. But as our conversations unfolded, it became clear that other mortals agreed with Tempest's claim that sin is not the absolute concept which is the bedrock of every angel's existence.

"Excuse me," the young woman said.

She was wearing close-fitting black jeans and a dark brown sweater that was woven from rough wool. She was thin but shapely in the way of youth and her eyes, though only brown, seemed to cover every shade from walnut to coffee.

"Yes?" I said.

"Are you Mr. Sinseeker?"

Immediately I saw that Tempest was attempting another ruse. He had sent this woman to cause mischief, to try to side-track my purpose.

"No," I said firmly. "My name is Angel. Joshua Angel." This was true. The name I used on earth was Joshua Angel.

"Oh," she said, showing no disappointment. She sat down next to me. "My friend wanted me to talk to this man Sinseeker for him. He said that he owes him some money, on a bet or somethin', and he wanted me to tell him that he had to wait till tomorrow to come and give it to him."

"Why couldn't your friend come himself?"

"My name is Branwyn Weeks," she said.

"Hello, Miss Weeks."

"You can call me Brownie. Everybody calls me Brownie, even my mama and she the one named me Branwyn. That's a Welsh name. My mama said that she thought it was so beautiful when she heard it that she just had to have a daughter and give her that name."

"It's beautiful," I found myself saying.

Branwyn smiled.

"Thank you," she said. "Are you waiting for somebody?"

"Yes."

"A girlfriend?"

"A man."

"Well, I guess we could wait together."

"I don't know how long I'll be here. I doubt if the man I'm waiting for will come."

"Why's that?" she asked.

I stalled at that question. So far I had not lied to this young woman. My name is not Sinseeker, though I have a seat in the heavenly choir and have served for thousands of years as the chief accounting angel for heaven's gate. And, though I was sure she had been sent by the wayward Tempest Landry, she had not used his name and therefore I did not truly know that she was looking for me.

But if I were to tell her the truth—that I believed Tempest was not coming because I suspected that he had sent her to somehow make me argue with her about the status of his soul—then I would put myself in the position of having to talk with her about Tempest.

If I lied and gave some excuse then Tempest would be able to argue that I myself was a sinner and how could a sinner send a sinner to hell?

Angels in heaven cannot lie. It is beyond them. But on earth I was in human guise and therefore had all of the abilities of mankind—lying being one of the most prominent.

"That's okay," Branwyn said. "You don't have to tell me anything."

She could tell, I supposed, that I was uncomfortable and showed me this small kindness. I was profoundly moved because it was a deep conflict of conscience, to lie or not, that I in all my millennia of existence had never faced before. She released me from a terrible burden because she had perceived the pain that the crafty Tempest Landry had set me up for.

"Are you okay?" Branwyn asked.

Still I could not speak.

"I just talk too much," she went on. "You know my mama

always said that if I could just keep quiet a little bit that I might learn something. My daddy used to tell me that he'd give me twenty dollars if I'd sit still and be quiet for five minutes. I'd say okay but you know words would start comin' outta my mouth before ten seconds went by."

Her words were like a cool breeze soothing the heat of my conflict. Her smile and brown-on-brown eyes looking into mine allowed me peace again.

"What's your friend's name?" I asked Branwyn Weeks.

"Tempest," she said. And before I could tell her that that was also the man I was to see, she went on, "He's a really nice man. I mean, I wouldn't go to meet some stranger that he owed money to unless I thought I owed him something too."

"What do you owe him?"

"My life," she said.

"He saved your life?"

"Just about," she said with a nod. "I mean he didn't push me out from in front of no car or nuthin' but I had got real sick after my boyfriend, my ex, beat on me and I didn't have no place to go and Tempest found me and give me food and money."

"What about your parents? Why didn't they help?"

"I was too ashamed to go to them. I was all beat up. Two front teeth broke out. And I was real, real skinny 'cause I had internal injuries and the food just went right through me. But Tempest took me to the hospital with a . . ." Branwyn paused and looked at me.

"With what?"

"Are you here for Tempest?" she asked.

"Yes."

"An' he owes you money?"

"There is a debt that we have to negotiate, yes."

"He bought an insurance card off of a pickpocket and used it to fool the hospital to think that the woman who had the card was me. He brought me in on a Friday so I could stay for four days before the finance office found out."

The beauty of Branwyn Weeks increased as her story unfolded. I felt sorry for her but at the same time angry at Tempest, but I was not quite sure why.

"I had a ruptured spleen and they operated and then Tempest took me home to my mama. The doctor in the hospital said that if I didn't get that operation I'da prob'ly died."

"Did you pay them back for the insurance you stole?" I asked. I didn't want to but I was an accounting angel after all.

Branwyn shook her head. "It cost sixteen thousand dollars and that ain't even with the room. I only make six twenty-nine a hour at my supermarket job. And if I tried to pay they might arrest me."

"It was Tempest who used the insurance card," I said. "It's him they would prosecute, I'm sure."

"But he saved my life."

It came clear to me then why Tempest angered me so. He was presenting me with a problem where sin existed but there was no simple identification of the sinner.

"What happened to your boyfriend, the one who beat you?" I asked.

"I don't know and I don't care. We lived in Brooklyn. I came to Manhattan after the last time he beat me. Tempest found me on the street not twelve blocks from here. And now I live up in Harlem, with three girls I met from work."

My breath was coming hard. I was supposed to be the one making arguments against Tempest but instead I found myself questioning the nature of sin. Branwyn was lovely and fragile and deserving of her life. Part of me cheered her deliverance while another voice cursed Tempest for manipulating both me and that child.

"Can Tempest come talk with you tomorrow?" Branwyn asked.

"Yes," I said.

We sat for a long time in silence and then one of us, I forget which, suggested dinner.

I had never been to a movie before. Branwyn took me to a film, I forget the name, about a group of beautiful young black men and women who fell in love and got angry over and over again.

I accompanied Brownie to her door because I was afraid that William, her abusive ex-boyfriend, might pop out of some dark doorway and hurt her if I wasn't there.

She kissed me at her apartment door, first with her lips and then her tongue. We kissed as we had been talking, softly on the surface, deep passion underneath. It was my first kiss, followed by many others.

"I share a room with a girl," she said. "I don't think she could sleep with you in my bed."

There were tears in my eyes. This for some reason caused her to smile.

"You wouldn't beat me, would you, Mr. Angel?" she asked.

"I've never held the post of avenging angel," I replied.

"Huh?"

"Not even a mild spanking," I assured her.

"A little spankin' ain't so bad."

I CAME DOWN WITH a fever overnight. I missed work and my meeting with Tempest the next day. Branwyn called me and when I told her I was sick she said she'd come take care of me if it was bad. I told her no, that I'd be better in a day or two and maybe we could get together then—and talk.

When I got off of the phone I cried for hours lamenting something, I knew not what, that I had lost.

THE WAKE

W E MET AT a large funeral parlor, at the services of a woman named Sojourner Hatfield, way up in Harlem. The dead woman was on display in an open casket at the front of the room. More than five hundred chairs were set out. About a third of these were already occupied. Tempest Landry had asked me to meet him at ten past seven, and he was already there when I arrived. The services, I found out, were set for seven thirty p.m.

"Hello, Angel," Tempest called to me. He was sitting at the back of the chapel, at the far end of the last row of chairs.

I went up to him and nodded my greeting. I tried to sit in the chair next to him but he waved for me to sit one seat apart.

"It's gonna get crowded and I'd like a little room for as long as it lasts," he explained.

Looking at the pamphlet passed out at the door, I said, "It says here that the late Mrs. Hatfield was ninety-two years old. From my experience a crowd of this many chairs rarely shows up for a man or woman this age unless they were famous or maybe infamous."

"Not this time," Tempest said solemnly.

"Why—" I began, but Tempest cut me off, asking, "What you think'a Branwyn?"

"She's a nice girl," I said.

"Woman, please," he said, gesturing with his hands. "No girlchild is put together like she is. Not on this earth."

"Why did you send her to meet me that day?" I asked.

"Because I thought she might make you see that when you live in the sin of this world you got to work that sin to try and do good." Tempest said all this with a smile.

"I was not convinced," I said.

And it was true. Tempest was manipulating the pain of others, as far as I was concerned, to save himself from an eternity of damnation. For all I knew, he had saved Branwyn just to throw her at me.

"You a hard man, Angel," Tempest replied. "Here I am tryin' just to make it in a life that ain't never been easy—I'm not sayin' it wasn't fun, I'm not sayin' I would like to forget my memories and be somebody else—but life has been hard. Hard as a diamond and not worth a cent. Here I am tryin' t'get by, tryin' t'help my fellow man an' myself at the same time and all the while I got heaven countin' my sins with no care at all about the sins done against me."

"Life is hard," I quoted, "a great man once said."

"Is it hard for you?"

It was, but I would not tell my mortal charge that. My time on earth had been extremely trying. In human form I was vulnerable to hunger, disease, exhaustion, and the numbing fatigue of daily labors. But the worst experience I had was the scarcity of time.

Time was an inexhaustible commodity on the heavenly plane. If something needed to be done, then it was done. If a

thought took an instant or a thousand years, or a thousand thousand years, it was no matter. But on earth every moment fled,
leaving you with desperation, frustration, and fear. I was late
for work, late for my target dates on projects. Time slipped past
me and I had no idea where it had gone.

I had already been on earth for eleven months, trying to
convince Tempest Landry of his sins. If he confessed, he would
be delivered into hell. I thought it would take but a moment of
my deep voice and my convincing words, but Tempest resisted
me and the months flew by.

And now there was Branwyn Weeks.

Tempest had saved her life, as I said, and sent her to me as
an example of his goodness. I rejected his personified argument
but she and I became friends. I saw her almost every day in
parks and libraries. Sometimes I'd meet her after work and see
her to her door. At that threshold we'd kiss. Sometimes she'd
hug me and touch my neck lightly with her tongue.

As an angel I'd never known physical love, and though I
resisted, she was in my mind more than heaven.

"Excuse me," someone said.

I looked around and saw a dark-faced woman all in black.
She wanted me to move over. I wondered why she didn't sit
somewhere else but then I saw that the chapel was full to over-
flowing. I moved next to my charge.

Tempest nodded and then looked toward the podium with
uncharacteristic seriousness. He wore a brown suit and held a
brown suede hat between his knees.

"Tempest," I said.

He silenced me with a gesture.

An elderly black woman who wore the purple robes of a
denomination that I did not recognize began the sermon.

She told of a woman who came out of the Deep South and

who lived a life of sacrifice and defiance; a woman who raised eight children and often took in her grandchildren and great-grandchildren and children that were no relation to her whatsoever. All through that time Sojourner Hatfield worked as a seamstress, a domestic, an illegal liquor distributor, a numbers runner, a minister, and a newsletter editor.

"Her church never had a roof but her children always had a bed," the woman in purple said. "That's the way she saw it—poverty was her religion but her family never wanted a day."

Tempest was crying. The whole assembly was crying. Men and women of all ages, even the children seemed to be concentrating on the words. I looked around and realized that everyone in the room was black, Negro. I wondered why a woman who was so greatly loved would have no one but black people to cry for her.

Tempest's tears grew and soon he was sobbing loudly. He dropped his hat and left it on the floor. He buried his head in his hands, the moisture of his sorrow cascading down upon his forlorn hat.

A young man wailed near the front of the chapel. A woman called out the Lord's name. Only the eyes of heaven, mine, remained dry.

"Sojourner Hatfield," the minister told us, "wrote this note from her deathbed only a week ago."

The minister brought out a crumpled piece of lined school paper and positioned glasses in front of her eyes.

Family, both of blood and of love, I know that I am dying and soon I will be gone. Cry for me one day, weep on the next, but after that let me go. Let me go. Because you know as long as I hear your pain I cannot leave this mortal veil. I love you all and if you love me then let me

*get on with the work I have in the next world. My bible
is for Mother Marybelle,*

The minister's voice broke for the first time,

*who I am sure is reading you these words. My body is
destined to be clay once again. But my soul is forever in
the heart of the Lord. He will take me in. He will take us
all. Good-bye, Martha and Henrietta, LeRoy and
Martin, and Lana Lee. And to all of you who I knew,
and all I didn't, the pain is almost over, there's freedom
just beyond.*

I was surprised at my own tears. I had seen billions of deaths
and never once had I cried.

Never once had you eyes, a voice in my head said. That voice
was me.

After the services Tempest joined the long line of people
giving condolences. When he came to the front he didn't move
on like the others but instead stayed holding the hands of an
elderly woman who was confined to a wheelchair. Tempest
knelt next to her talking for more than an hour. I was reminded
of his time in front of Judge Peter. He broke protocol there
too.

At the front of the chapel, long after everyone else had gone,
Tempest bid farewell to the crippled woman, allowing the
young woman who helped her to roll the wheelchair away. The
old woman kissed Tempest on the cheek when he bowed to say
good-bye.

He was caressing that cheek when I came up to him.

"Not now, Angel," he said. "I don't want to hear it. I don't
wanna discuss what you call my sins. Sojourner Hatfield was

too good to get old and die like that. She was certainly too good to be judged by anybody but those who she touched."

"I'm sure she will ascend," I said.

"To cure evil," Tempest said, crying once again, "you gotta live with it. You gotta breathe it and eat it. You gotta call it brother, sleep by its side. Auntie Hatfield had a whole trunkful'a evil 'fore she turned it around. By your numbers she might be a sinner but the people in this room know better than you."

I could see the deep pain and loss in Tempest. I knew that he would never admit to sin in that state.

"All right," I said. "We don't have to continue our talk today but I would like to ask you a question."

"What?"

"Who was that woman you were talking to?"

"That was Hester. She's the head of the Landry clan."

"You were related?"

"She's my great-aunt."

"You know that she will not know you as her relation," I said.

"I said that I knew Sojourner and I told her things only somebody close could have known."

"You lied," I condemned.

"I did not," Tempest said. "But if I had it would'a been fine. You the one pick me up and tried to damn me, then put me in a body that even my own mother don't know how to love. I'm havin' dinner with Hester on Sunday next. After all these years of death and solitude I can finally be back with the family I love."

"You are not here to rebuild your old life," I said. "These moments given you are to accept your sins and their conse-quences."

"No," Tempest said. "That's your job. Mines is to live."

"You don't think that it's wrong for you to misrepresent yourself to your great-aunt?"

"I'm not misrepresentin' nuthin'. Everything I told her was true," Tempest growled. "I loved old Auntie Hatfield and she did tell me many things. Her death hurts me deep down inside. And I'm leavin' now because I told you that I would not argue about sin at this funeral."

"If you didn't want us to talk, why did you ask me to come?"

"You are my enemy, Angel," Tempest said, looking into my eyes. "You want me to fall and enter into hell. You hound me and try to trick me and even hate me for resisting your words. But still, you're my only friend. The only one who knows me. The only one who can speak my name and remember before I died."

Tempest was about to cry again and so he left me there in the chapel. The coffin was still at the front of the room.

I went up to gaze upon the tiny and frail body of the woman who touched so many. It wasn't her but only the clay she'd mentioned in her letter. I thought about Branwyn then. I wanted her to kiss me and I didn't know why.

A New Morning

I HAD BEEN THINKING about Branwyn for days; ever since attending the funeral of Sojourner Hatfield. The sorrow and loss that Tempest felt, that everyone in his extended family felt, at the death of that woman set off a longing in me.

It had something to do with the body I had to inhabit in order to manifest myself in the corporeal realm. As an angel I felt nothing about death. Death to the Infinite is a beginning, not an end. But life had changed all that. The loss of a single life had moved me more than fifty thousand years of death. My heart ached in sympathy with Tempest even though I was still committed to making him accept hell as his fate.

But I hadn't been thinking about Tempest. I hadn't been thinking about heaven or the heavenly choir. All that was on my mind was Branwyn Weeks; her delicate eyes and warm lips. I wanted her to hold me to her breast.

I may be the first angel ever to experience the stirrings of physical love. I held myself back. We had only kissed and rubbed up against each other—my heart, and other organs—yearning for more.

Many evenings she asked me to come in. Her roommates had given her the single bedroom and I was invited to spend the night.

I always demurred. I wasn't on earth to satisfy basic animal instincts. I came to reclaim the wayward soul of Tempest Landry and return to a repaired heaven as it loomed eternally over the fate of all life.

Every night I laid in bed, eyes wide open, heart throbbing loud enough to dispel any chance of slumber. Time and again I would get out of bed, don my trousers, shirt, and shoes. I'd go to the door, no matter the hour, intending to go to her, to beg her to hold me. But at the threshold a psalm would enter my mind, a peaceful chant that we angels sing while souls march on toward their fates. It was a psalm of blind piety. Most who heard it were made unaware of their fellow petitioners; they walked that last mile contemplating their sins. I don't know if the song came from a part of my heart that did not want to wallow in the corruption of the body, or if Peter himself sent it to me to keep me on the right path—but I had not in ten days gone to Branwyn. I did not go to her, call her, or answer her calls.

One day, however, the psalm did not come. Maybe it did but I had turned on the radio to try and lull myself to sleep. The radio did not calm me, however, and I arose and dressed. When I reached the door, a man was singing about an undying love. It was this magic of pain I needed to pass outside.

It was well after midnight when I reached Branwyn's door in Harlem. I rang the bell and knocked too.

A minute or more passed and I almost turned away. If only he had waited a few seconds more I would have been gone. But he came to the door dressed only in boxer shorts.

"What the hell you doin' here?" Tempest Landry asked me.

"I came to . . ." My words trailed off when I realized that Tempest might have been there with the woman I loved.

"I mean you ain't never said nuthin' 'bout climbin' into my bed," Tempest was saying.

Branwyn came into view of the doorway. She was wearing a short night dress and her hair was tousled.

I began to cry.

"What you doin' now?" Tempest demanded.

I turned and ran down the hallway, my shoulders colliding with the walls as I went.

"Joshua, don't go!" Branwyn shouted.

I fell down the first flight of stairs and stumbled down the rest.

Out in the street I was lost. I walked with no destination. There was a slight mist in the air.

Angels have no eyes in their original form but they express sorrow that the Infinite compares to tears. An angel's sorrow is only evoked, it is said, in sadness at the state of the human race. I cried that night over my own pain. The evil trickster Tempest had finally defeated me by turning my own heart against the logic of heaven.

I HAD PLANNED TO tell him at our next meeting that he had won, that all the aeons of sanctity and safety for the soul of mankind had been rent asunder by his callous desire to escape punishment for his sins. I believed this because it came to me in a vision that once one soul refused the decree of heaven, soon the line drawn between good and evil would vanish and the universe would be chaos.

For a month that calamity was put off because neither Tempest nor I would speak to the other. Branwyn called me but I did not answer her.

Six weeks and three days after I ran from Branwyn's door I got a call at work.

"Mr. Angel," Pippa Meyers called over the intercom.

"Yes."

"It's a call for you."

"Hello," I said into my headset's microphone.

"Hey, Angel," his voice rang in my ear.

My first impulse was to rip the headset off and crush it under my foot. But the violence of the thought shocked me so much that I couldn't accomplish the goal.

"What do you want?" I said instead.

"Meet me at the inside dining court at Citicorp at six," he said and hung up.

CITICORP'S DINING COURT WAS a series of tables at the heart of the building. Some arcane city ordinance made the builders create a place where pedestrians could go. It was like a public square where high school children, homeless drifters, and tired secretaries stopped from time to time.

Tempest was already there when I arrived at six fifteen.

"You're late," he said as I pulled up a chair to the small round table.

"The subway was slow," I said.

"Well what do you know," he replied, "an angel with an excuse."

My hands balled into fists and I imagined striking Tempest. Sin had taken me over.

"She's mine," he said. "Why you wanna mess with that?"

"She belongs to no one," I declared.

"I don't remember in no history book that you come down from heaven and freed the black folks when the white man had them in chains. How come you gonna free Branwyn?"

"You're the one who sent her to me," I said, loud enough that heads turned from around the room.

"To prove to you that I was a good man, even though I have to do wrong sometimes, to make good work."

"To prove to me that you used that poor child when she was down and dying just so that you would not have to suffer the flames of hell."

"That's not it and you know it," Tempest said. "All my life I been helpin' people need help when I could. A lotta times it was me that needed but it's always the same thing. I fight when I'm threatened, when I'm loved, I love back."

"She was beaten and bleeding and you took her in so that she could come to me. You knew when you sent her that I'd fall in love and lose my head. That's why you slept with her. You did it because you knew that it would strain my vows."

"Love?" Tempest said in an awed tone.

At first I didn't remember using the word. Angels love all beings, large and small. But the love I professed was different. It was personal. I was a person. Tears sprouted in my eyes again. Tempest was shaking his head in amazement.

"I thought you said that you was an angel," he said.

"I am. I am, but I am also a man. I'm here to converse with you. In the form of an angel I cannot talk, only command. Even in this guise my voice holds authority. But it must be your choice to accept your sins and so I can only speak to you as a fellow mortal. But as a mortal I am as open to sin as you."

"And you call love a sin?"

"Not so much sin as malingering. I have a purpose that's higher than human congress."

"Did you sleep with her?" Tempest asked.

"In my mind I can think of nothing else. It doesn't matter whether I have or haven't; I want to and that is my crime."

"Maybe it don't matter to you but it do to me, so I'ma ask you again—did you sleep with her?"

"Why do you care about what I've done? In your life of sin you slept with many women who were married. Would you answer that question if someone asked it of you?"

"You know I been in her bed 'cause you seen me in her house. But she went after you when you ran and then she told me she had to be alone. I thought that it was because she knew you were an angel. I thought maybe she thought that she was sinnin' with me. Not that you was jealous but that you would damn her soul."

"Do you love her?" I asked.

Tempest hesitated, not his usual trait. He bit his lower lip and lowered his eyelids. He rubbed the moisture from his lips and said, "I don't know. She's nice and she needs me. She the first one that has cared about me since I come back alive."

"So we're the same," I said.

"How you see that?"

"We're both afraid of love but unable to turn away."

For a moment longer than any in heaven Tempest and I stared at each other. I had never been further from divinity than I was at that moment.

After that Tempest Landry did smile.

"You laugh?" I said.

"Well don't you think it's funny? An angel and a wayward soul stopping for love on the path to hell? I've had what you want and I want her to run after me like she ran after you."

I couldn't hold back the giggle in my throat. Tempest smiled and I did too.

"If you break my resolve and I confess my sins," Tempest said, "then you will shed this skin and return without knowing love."

The truth of his words crushed the flesh heart in my chest.

"If I don't," Tempest continued, "then I have a rival for the only woman I've truly cared about in two lifetimes."

It isn't fair, a voice in my head said.

"I could command you to hell," I said.

Tempest said a word that I cannot repeat.

"It is true," I said. "I have the power to damn you. But no angel has ever used that power because men have always followed our decrees."

"Like children," Tempest spat. "Well I ain't a child, I'm a man."

And so was I. And even though I had told the truth, I could damn his soul to hell, I wasn't sure how that act would change the balance of good and evil. I was loath to break him or leave the earth at all.

"So," he said. "We continue our talks? Or do you end it right here with that big boomin' voice?"

"We continue."

"I'ma keep on seein' Branwyn," Tempest said.

"So will I."

"We gonna make a man outta you yet, angel-baby."

"We," I said, "shall do the same for you."

GONE FISHIN'

THE MORNING AIR was chill and brisk, like nothing I had ever felt before. Gulls wheeled and cried in the skies above us while the ocean's dull roar made even my voice seem small.

"Throw it overhead," Tempest was saying.

He was trying to show me how to use a fishing rod, casting the line into the surf.

"Like this?" I cried.

"No, no, no. Use your wrist not your shoulder. You're not playin' ball."

He'd already caught a few small fish that he kept wet in a pail of water.

"I don't think I'll ever get it," I said.

"It ain't that hard, just snap your wrist and keep your arm straight."

That time I got it right. My hook went out beyond a breaking wave and stayed in the water, trawling for fish.

"Are you angry with me?" I asked Tempest.

"'Bout what?"

"About me still seeing Branwyn even though you want her for yourself."

"Have you slept with her?"

I had not but I said, "I've decided that that's not information that I should share with you."

"You haven't," Tempest said while throwing his line back in. "If you did you'd be talkin' differently and so would she—in my bed."

Every time he alluded to his sexual relationship with the woman I loved, a rage bored its way through my body.

Love for me was a totally unexpected thing. After all I am an angel, even on earth, more spirit than man. But the body I inhabited to convince Tempest Landry of his sins was susceptible to all things human, including love, hatred, and pain.

"I don't care to hear about your relationship with Branwyn. Her time, when she's not with me, is her own."

"You see," Tempest said, "that must be the difference between a angel and a man. I get mad even knowin' that you out to dinner with her; that she says when she sees you at night she won't see me until at least the next day. Man, if I thought you was gettin' some action I might have to lay siege on heaven itself."

"Why don't we return to our discussions?" I suggested. "It's been some time since we've discussed your sins."

"Not my sins," Tempest corrected, "but the damnation of my soul for just tryin' to make it in a world where you got me by the short hairs and holdin' me over a cliff."

"We have no control over you life," I replied. "You are a free agent, at liberty to take any actions you wish."

"That's a good one."

"What do you mean?"

"You tellin' me that you ain't got no control. If you ain't got it, then who does? I was born in a two-room apartment with three brothers, four sisters, a mother, and a long line'a men— any one'a which could have been my old man. I got white cops callin' me nigger and a school that's a joke. I was hungry more than I wasn't as a child and I had to have eyes all over my head. I been butted and battered, kicked and stabbed too. All that and I never asked for a bit of it and you sayin' it's my fault."

"The challenges you faced in life were opportunities," I said, "opportunities to do right."

"How can you say that?"

"It has been the truth for over a hundred thousand years of humanity."

"Maybe true for you, but up there in heaven you didn't even know the meanin' of pain. Down here if I made a mistake an' got this barb in your eye you'd be mad enough to kill me. Now tell me if I'ma lie."

"I would not kill you."

"But would you hit me?"

"If . . . if I did it would be a sin."

"But if even a angel could be tempted, then how do you expect me to be better?"

"Temptation is not the problem, it is the act that is the sin."

"What about those cops that killed me?" Tempest asked.

"We've discussed them already."

"I wanna come at it one more time."

"What about them?" I asked patiently, and tossed my line again.

"They shot me, right?"

"You know they did."

"Killed me dead even though I was innocent as a lamb."

"Innocent of the crime they sought you for."

"All I was doin' was listenin' to my music, mad that the mini disc player wasn't playin' right," Tempest said. "I did make a quick gesture but that was throwing the player downward, away from me with my back turned. You couldn't mistake that for a man tryin' to shoot at you."

"Agreed."

"But they shot me, killed me with over a dozen bullets. They hurt me and my mother, my wife, my girlfriend, my children, and my friends. They robbed me of the chance of changing the balance of my sins—"

"So you agree that you were a sinner?" I asked. "That the decree of heaven was sound?"

Tempest reeled in his line. There was a silvery almost triangular-shaped fish on his hook. Tempest held the line and watched the fish struggle for a moment, then he freed it from the hook and threw it back in. I remember thinking, the shepherd and the fisherman, without attaching any meaning to the phrase.

My heart thrilled from fear and expectation because if Tempest said yes at that moment, our souls would have both fled the earth. He would descend to the nether realm of hell and I would return to the mount of heaven—never to know love at all.

"I agree," said Tempest, "that we are all sinners—me included. But the judgment of heaven has not been proved to my satisfaction."

I hoped that my sigh went unheard under the ocean's din.

"What I was sayin'," Tempest continued, "was that if I were a sinner destined for hell those cops cut off my chances for eternal bliss. They cut down a living man before he could maybe change his ways."

"Such is the way of life," I said sagely.

"But it's not fair."

"Life isn't fair."

"Why not?" Tempest asked with none of his usual guile.

"That is the way of the world," I said.

"But if the world is the product of heaven and man is made to overcome his evil, then why don't he have all the time he needs? Why would he have to be cut down and destroyed just because some cop cain't tell one black man from the other? Why they can kill me and you want 'em in heaven, when I'm the one killed, and I go to hell?"

"Who is to say that they are heaven bound?"

"You could say," Tempest said.

He was right.

"Three of the four, if they died today, would gain the kingdom tomorrow," I said.

"Three murderers get forever vacation with pay, and the man they killed, a man who ain't never killed no one, gets thrown in the pit 'cause they killed him before his time."

"It is not for you to judge another," I said. The words made a hollow sound in the curve of a wave.

"Didn't they judge me?"

"I don't see how."

"They saw me, figured me for a thief, shot me dead, and left me, body and soul, to rot. I didn't have a chance and you know that's not right. So why cain't I make a judgment on them? Why cain't I say it was wrong?"

"Don't you see, Tempest?" I said. "There is a greater purpose. Something beyond your simple complaint. While we stand here arguing, the firmament quakes. Your refusal to accept judgment could disrupt eternity."

"Maybe that's why I'm here," Tempest replied. "Maybe I'm supposed to question what has come before."

"You are nothing," I said.

"So then who are you here talkin' to—the wind?"

For a long time after that we didn't speak. I threw in my line as well as he but I caught no fish. Tempest's bucket was filled with the flipping fins of his catch.

When the sun was halfway to noonday he jammed the butt of his rod into the sand and sat down. I joined him.

"You see that bucket?" he said.

"A good day's catch," I agreed.

"No. Not at all. Look in there. All them fish, half starved for the air in the water."

They were packed in closely but most were still alive.

"What about them?" I asked.

"That's the way you got us down here on the earth. Fish almost outta water and here you want 'em in church. Cain't move at all, can hardly breathe but you want 'em to gasp out prayer. That's the prison I could be in. That's the ghetto where I live."

Tempest stood and went down to the water. He threw the fish into the ocean, bucket and all. Some of them I could see were nearly dead but many flitted away.

"Why did you do that?" I asked.

"You don't know?"

I shook my head.

"Maybe you really don't," Tempest speculated. "Which means ignorance rules the world."

I DROVE US BACK to Manhattan in the car I had rented. Tempest didn't understand me. Nor did I understand him. I wondered what would happen when we spoke the same words.

BOMBARDIER

TEMPEST WAS WORKING at a restaurant on Broad Street down in the financial district. When he got off at two a.m. I was waiting outside the front door to greet him.

"What are you doin' here?" he asked me.

"I wanted to continue our talk," I said. "We were doing so well I wanted to go on."

"Man, I just don't get it. Here it seems to me that you don't understand a word I'm sayin' and there you are poppin' up in the middle'a the night wantin' to hear some more."

"You agreed that you have sinned," I said. "That the reason you were condemned in heaven is because the police ended your life too soon."

Tempest stopped walking and turned to me.

"No," he said. "Heaven misjudged me and the cops murdered me on behalf of the state. Everybody sins, even you when you wear a body. Man is a sinner but that don't make him bad."

Tempest turned on his heel and walked at a fast clip. I kept up with him though, happy that I had gotten under his thick skin.

"But you must admit," I said, "the police aren't on trial here."

"The police ain't never on trial," Tempest protested. "And if they are, then the judge and jury are just happy to believe whatever they say. A cop on the witness stand is like you angels up in heaven, nobody questions your words or deeds neither. But me on the other hand, I couldn't do right if I tried. Nobody believes me. I'm just a lie waiting to happen. After thirty-four years of bein' made into a lie they shot me down and sent me to you and you said I should enter into hell."

"That's not what happened," I said. "You're twisting the events to make it seem like the whole world is in a conspiracy against you."

"And ain't it?" Tempest asked. "Ain't it so? The police ready to shoot me. The courts want me in jail. I'm makin' just enough to keep off the landlord, but food and clothes takin' turns at my wallet. I'm an American, at least I was before I died; a citizen of the greatest, most powerful country in the history of the world. A citizen mind you, not no slave or visitor or foreigner to this shore. My people been here longer than most, way back over four hundred years. And we built without salary and we died without our right names. We are part of the stone and blood of this nation. How can it be that we strugglin' like this? Livin' with drugs and prejudice, shot down, dragged down, sat on, and lied to. If that ain't conspiracy, then I don't know what it is."

"Nobody planned it this way, Tempest," I argued. "You must admit that."

"Who needs a plan when you can shoot us like fish in a barrel? Who needs a blueprint when we don't have a choice where to live? Them ccps didn't need to lay in wait for me. They loose and armed in my neighborhood twenty-four seven."

"So your excuse is race?" I said. "That and nothing more?"

"It's not just race, Angel. No it ain't that only. There's brown skins and yellow skins and white ones too that share my fate. It's poor men and angry ones, fatherless and motherless and homeless ones too. No, it's not just race but still, a black man got a anchor 'round his neck and a bull's-eye on his back. Other peoples got problems too, but excuse me if I suffer alone."

"Many, many people survive," I countered. "Many climb out of the ghetto and other grim circumstances. Thousands from your own generation have been faced with odds greater than you've encountered and they've accounted themselves nobly."

Again Tempest stopped walking. This time he looked angry enough to strike me.

"When I was a boy there was a nut in my high school," he said in an exceptionally calm tone. "He was a genius but he was crazy. Liked to play with fire and get stoned. One day in science class he brought in a cardboard box with wires stickin' out all over the place. It was his project, he told the teacher, a time bomb."

"I don't believe it," I said.

"That a black kid would make a time bomb? Or that he'd lie and say that he did?"

"That you were ever in a science class. Don't forget, I am your accounting angel, I know everything about you."

"Well, you're right about the classroom. I wasn't in there. But I was at school that day. I heard the story like everybody else."

"Then go on," I said.

"This kid, Vincent Moldin, had the box up front. He had never turned in homework or finished a quiz or test, so the teacher thought it was just some retarded joke. Then Vincent said, How do you grade a bomb's insides if it blows up to prove it's a bomb? The teacher got mad and told Vincent to sit down. Then Vincent got mad and grabbed at his box. The heck if it wasn't a bomb and it blew up right there. Set the natural gas for the Bunsen burners on fire. Two kids burned to death right in their chairs. A lotta others were scarred and maimed." Tempest began walking again, his thoughts lost in that long-ago explosion.

"What does Vincent Moldin have to do with you blaming racism for your sins?" I asked.

"Not Vincent Moldin but Harold Gee."

"I thought that it was Vincent Moldin who made the bomb."

"It was. But Harold was sitting right there next to him, right in the first row. Vincent was blinded, lost his left hand. Almost every child in that room had a busted eardrum and some kinda concussion and wound. But Harold came out of it with nary a scratch. When that bomb blew up, the force missed Harry. He picked up and ran from the room."

Tempest stopped there, shaking his head in sorrow at the pain of his classmates.

"So?" I asked. "What does that story mean?"

"Don't you get it?"

"No."

"You walkin' there next to me in the middle'a the night after I done worked fourteen hours washin' dishes for change. You askin' me why ain't I like the few that crawled out from the slime but you won't even hear what I got to say."

"I don't understand what you mean."

"What did Harold do when he found himself whole after the blowup?"

"He ran, you said."

"That's right. He didn't stop to face the fire or drag his friends from the room. He didn't call for the principal or look for Vincent's hand. If he'da done that, he would have been caught in the aftershock of the gas that ignited from the flames the bomb made."

"You can't compare running from an explosion with a man or woman educating themselves and rising from poverty," I said.

"I can and I do," Tempest replied. "To begin with, no one educates himself. Anyone that says that they did is either stupid or a lie. How can you learn without a book? How can you want to learn without food in your stomach and a mother's love? How can you know you right if every time you say somethin' somebody hits you and says to shut up? I don't blame Harold for runnin' but I don't call him a hero for it neither. He was lucky and he was quick. That's all you can ask for in the battlefield of black America. And if you get away, more power to ya. But please don't tell me I should follow your lucky feet."

"You pervert the truth, my friend," I said. "Many people stay. They work in the community, they help the less fortunate."

"If they stay, then they feel the aftershock, you could bet your feathers on that."

We had reached the subway station. It was desolate at Bowling Green. The wary clerk in the token booth watched us closely as we went to wait for the train.

"You must admit it, Tempest," I said. "Some people have made a life for themselves without resorting to sin."

"Have you ever passed such a person into heaven? A man who never sinned?"

"No. But ones whose sins were negligible. Ones whose virtues outweighed their sins a thousand to one."

"Many poor fellas like that?"

"As many as the rich."

"I don't believe it."

"But it's true," I said.

"You got statistics on that?"

"No. No, but I know human nature."

"If you knew human nature you wouldn't be here tryin' to convince me of my sins. I'm sayin' that I believe that a poor man has to resort to sin a lot quicker than a man who ain't poor. Just like a man scared for his life don't have time to waste when he's runnin' from a bomb."

"We don't care about wealth in heaven."

"Rich kids never do. How can you care about somethin' when you always had it. It's like skin. You don't value it unless half gets burned off in a explosion in science class."

"Why are you so angry, Tempest?"

"Didn't I just tell you that I'm comin' off of a fourteen-hour shift? I'm tired and I got to go to work tomorrow and they won't understand it if I say I want a nap."

"So you're going to bed?"

"With Branwyn," he said behind a wolfish grin.

"But you said you're upset."

"That's what a good woman's for. She take her man's anger in both hands and squeeze it till it go down."

Tempest knew how to get to me. Every time I thought of Branwyn and him I got angry enough to fight.

"You got to blow off steam, Angel," Tempest said. "Try it sometimes. You might see sin in a whole new light."

The No. 4 train pulled up just then. The doors opened and Tempest stepped in.

"Ain't you comin'?" he asked.

"I want to think about what we've said tonight."

He smiled and nodded. The door closed on his smile.

As the train bore him away I wondered, not for the first time, if Tempest was a spy sent from below to test the resolve of heaven.

ETERNAL LOVE

SHE WAS WAITING at my door the next day after work. She wore a close-fitting green sweater and a short leather skirt. Her lips were red and her eyes were happy to see me. My human heart jerked so violently that for a moment I worried that I might die then and there.

"Hi, Joshua," she said, using my earthly name.

"Brownie," I replied, using the nickname for Branwyn.

"Can I talk to you?"

"About what?"

"Can we go in your place?"

We were both breathing hard. I knew that I should send her away but instead I worked my key on the door and gestured for her to go before me.

She sat on my sofa. I sat in the chair opposite.

"Can I have some water?" she asked.

I went to the kitchen to get her a glass.

When I returned she patted the cushion next to her, and I, like an obedient child, sat where she wanted me to.

"Did Tempest send you?" I asked.

"No. He wouldn't be happy that I came."

"I don't see why," I said in a tone that was new to me. "You see him almost every night, at least that's what he says."

"And why shouldn't I?" she said, suddenly angry. "Ain't nobody said nuthin' else to me. Ain't nobody else askin' to be with me."

"I didn't mean—"

"I do see him almost every night," she said with tears welling in her eyes. "We go out to movies and dancing, he buys me perfume and chocolates. He'd make love to me till morning if I wanted but he never push it that far 'cause he know I need my sleep. And in the morning he makes coffee and walks me to the bus stop and waves me off to work."

By the end of the list of Tempest's virtues Branwyn was crying on my shoulder.

"Why are you crying?" I asked her. "It all sounds wonderful. He's treating you like you deserve."

At that she wailed and cried harder. I put my arms around her to keep her from shivering.

"What's wrong?" I asked. "Don't you love Tempest?"

"Yes, I love him. He saved my life. He's sweet and he's funny and he knows what I'm talking about when I only say two or three words." She took time to breathe in and cry some more. "He's good with my little cousins when I have to babysit and he never hit me even once. He'd be a great father and husband."

I wondered if Tempest had told Branwyn about the power I held over his life; that I was trying to get him to resign his soul to eternal damnation, accepting the fate decreed by the Infinite. Even if he told her some story about me representing the government or something like that, she might be at my door trying to convince me to leave him alone.

"So why are you here instead of with him?" I asked her.

"Because every time we're dancing, I close my eyes and think about you. Because every time he nods and understands me I think of how you get that silly look like you just don't know. Because late at night when he squeeze me and say, what's my name? I have to think hard not to call out for you 'cause you on my mind every day and night. I been with Tempest every night for the last two weeks. Every day it gets better but every day I want you more."

She looked up at me then and all the voices of heaven, voices that had been in my mind every moment for a hundred thousand years, went silent. Suddenly I was helpless and alone. There was no belief or power that could tear me away from that kiss. Something fierce and angry rose up into my chest and went after her sweet offering like a wild beast. I was crying and so was she.

Time passed like the eternal hours of heaven.

We didn't leave my house for three days. She was fired from her job and my bosses were on the verge of letting me go. I lamented my fall but there was no other choice. I never suspected the sweet pain of love. The kisses that stung, the sore muscles and aching heart. She was there next to me but that wasn't enough. I needed her to tell me that she would never leave, that no man ever meant to her what I did.

Every now and then I even forgot that I was an angel. I didn't care about Tempest or Peter or the fate of the world. All that mattered was her lips saying my name.

The day she left for her mother's birthday party I almost cried. I kept stopping her for another kiss and the promise that she would return.

"I have to call Tempest," she said.

"Why?"

"I have to tell him that I'm with you now."

"Don't you think he already knows?"

"He saved my life. I owe him that."

I went in to work worrying that Tempest would seduce her once they talked on the phone. He'd say that they should meet to discuss it. Then he would kiss her and his kisses would be more experienced than mine. They would go to his place or hers to talk but talking would lead to loving and I'd be the one alone.

My boss, Grantman Chin, called me into his office.

"If you can't be counted on we'll have to let you go," he said.

"I've worked hard for you this past year," I answered. "If I can't miss a few days at work for private business, then maybe I should leave."

I knew he would back down. I was the best accountant they ever had. In the back of my mind I knew that it was unbecoming of an angel to be rude to a mortal man as I was to him. But at six o'clock when Branwyn came to meet me I didn't care about anything except the love in our hearts. "What did Tempest say?" I asked her over a glass of red wine at a hotel bar on Forty-sixth.

"He just was kinda quiet. He said he thought it was somethin' like that and got off the phone."

"Did he want to see you?"

"Uh-uh. No. He just said that he'd see us around and hung up. I called him back but he didn't pick up the phone."

I DIDN'T CARE ABOUT Tempest. He could live out his whole life and I could do the same with Branwyn. When it was all over we'd die and ascend to heaven and we'd have all of eternity to feel our deep love.

Six weeks went by, and then seven, eight. Branwyn got a job at a cut-rate pharmacy and I continued my accounting and loving her smile. We were still in love but the hunger for each other had lessened a bit. Two or three nights a week I spent at home alone.

One evening there was a letter in my mailbox. It had come from Atlanta, which surprised me because I knew no one outside of work besides Tempest and Branwyn.

> *Dear Angel,*
>
> *I never thought that I would talk to you again. I was mad. Real mad at you. You know I love Branwyn more than any woman I ever knew. She's the only woman in my life. When she called and told me that she chose you over me my heart was like that egg when they say that it's your brain on drugs.*
>
> *I think it was dying made me more open to a woman. Dying made me realize how precious my life is. That's why I saved Branwyn and befriended so many people since I been back.*
>
> *But when she told me that you and her was together I lost it. I tried my best but she still turned to you.*
>
> *In my mind I thought that she was the one who was supposed to make the decision about my soul. If she loved me and stayed with me I would know that I would stand up against heaven and stay in the world. But when she turned away I figured that it was all lost, that I would admit my sins and face the music. And if I did that they'd condemn me but also they'd send your butt back up into heaven.*
>
> *I was happy because the same call that broke my*

heart would also take away the love that beat me. Branwyn would lose you because she damned me.

So I did like you always do to me. I went down to your house and waited for you to come home from work. I was waiting at that little park down the street from your apartment building's door. I waited there for hours and then I saw you walking up the hill. My heart was filled with mean feelings that I ain't felt since before I was murdered. I was gonna go up to you and confess my sins but Branwyn shouted your name and run up the hill after you as fast as she could. I could see that she was winded but she kissed you anyway and you picked her up in the air. Both of you looked goofy. You held hands and grinned and walked all crooked like a ship on a rocky sea.

Branwyn looked so happy that I smiled just a little. That was when I knew that I couldn't hurt her. And when I knew that, I realized that all this time I've been right and I don't deserve damnation.

Maybe you agree with me now that you have her in your bed. I bet you forgot heaven for a few seconds there.

Anyway, I'm in Georgia now but I won't be here long. I'm traveling around the country to see how other black folks are doing. I haven't given up our talks about sin. I'll come back to New York sooner or later. You ain't seen the last of me.

Say good-bye to Brownie for me. Tell her I hope you two do okay.

Best wishes,
Tempest Landry

While reading his letter heaven flooded back into my heart. I saw, as maybe only an angel can, that Tempest had been saved. But the moment came too late. Heaven had sentenced him and it was my job to carry out that dictum.

But I was happy that he had fled. In my mortal guise I could not find him and so, I'd have to wait for his return—with Branwyn in my arms.

THE APPLE

Awe and Dread

THAT EARLY THURSDAY was no different than any other weekday morning in the past three months. I kissed the sleeping Branwyn, my mortal lover. She opened her eyes and smiled for me. Our baby, Tethamalanianti, cooed and then cried. I took the baby from the crib, changed her diaper, brought her to my first love's breast, and we sat together watching the sunrise from our Staten Island apartment window.

"You are my perfect angel," Branwyn said. "Isn't he, Titi?"

For uncounted thousands of years I had heard these words spoken on high but for some reason her opinion meant more to me than that of the entire heavenly choir.

"I have to go to work," I said, and my brown-skinned lover pouted as she did every morning.

"You could stay home one day," she said.

I kissed her forehead and Titi's nose.

"I've got to pay the rent," I said.

I TOOK THE STATEN Island Ferry across to Battery Park and then the Westside No. 1 train to Forty-second Street. On

Fortieth, behind the library, I went into a slender building and up to floor thirteen. There I unlocked the door of Rendell, Chin, and Mohammed tax accountants and bookkeepers for small businesses. The RCM accounting firm recognized my abilities and in the past year had promoted me to manager.

For centuries I had been the accounting angel for the keeper of the gate of heaven. The keeper had changed over time and the souls that beheld him on the final Judgment Day called him by various names depending on their earthly faith, but I had known him for the past two thousand years as St. Peter.

To everyone I knew, everyone who beheld my visage, I was a mortal man, Joshua Angel. I seemed to be in my thirties, male, and Negro. I had been in this guise for two years, six months, and nine days by earthly reckoning. Tempest Landry had died from an accidental shooting when the New York police mistook him for an armed and fleeing felon.

Even considering the tragic circumstances of Tempest's death, Peter saw fit to condemn him to hell. But, for the first time in the history of the Infinite, a mortal soul—Tempest— refused to accept this judgment and therefore caused great consternation in heaven.

What if more mortals refused? The whole system might crumble.

"MR. ANGEL," CATHERINE LAWTON said, breaking my midmorning reverie.

"Yes?"

"A courier left this letter for you."

The chubby young woman handed me a small envelope with the name *Angel* scrawled upon it.

The envelope wasn't sealed. I took out a slip of paper. And read it.

Hey Angel,

Come meet me down in Bryant Park.
                                   Tempest

My tongue went immediately dry and my heart began to flutter madly. These sensations were wholly new to me but I knew that they were symptoms of dread. Tempest was back and wanted to talk. If I succeeded in turning him to the ways of heaven he would enter immediately into hell and I would be drawn back to my celestial post. Branwyn and Tethamalanianti would be lost to me forever. I wanted to run away, to escape from this hard fate. I had never felt love like I had for Branwyn. And then, when Titi was born, my joy was so great that it knew no bounds. It felt like sin, it was so powerful, but I knew that it was love.

Miss Lawton cleared her throat.

"Was there anything else, Cathy?" I asked.

"You have a beautiful baritone voice, Mr. Angel."

"Thank you."

"We have an interdenominational choir down in Battery Park that meets on Wednesday nights. Do you like to sing?"

"Sing?" I said. "I was born singing."

"Would you—" she began.

"I have to go," I said, cutting her off.

HE WAS SITTING ON a bench next to another man at the center of the block-sized park. I was relieved that he had brought someone along. That meant he intended to continue our banter, that he wasn't quite ready to give up the ghost and accept his fate.

I found it odd that the man he sat with was white. Tempest didn't seem to like, or trust, white people very much. The white

man was young, in his twenties, and beautiful by earthly standards. He wore a black T-shirt and black slacks with reddish
brown snakeskin shoes. On the baby finger of his left hand he
wore a pinky ring set with a deep red gem—probably a ruby.

Tempest for his part was well dressed. His charcoal gray suit
was very stylish, with three buttons down the front. His shirt
was yellow and a good-sized yellow diamond, anchored in plat-
inum, adorned his baby finger.

"Angel," Tempest hailed with a big smile on his face. He
rose and took my hand warmly. "It's good to see you," he said.

I shook his hand.

"Where have you been, Tempest?" I asked.

"Come on," he replied, "sit down. Meet my friend Bob."

The elegantly underdressed white man stood and extended
a hand. He beamed at me, saying, "It's a pleasure to meet you,"
with a slight southern drawl.

I nodded, meeting his eyes, which, despite his grin, were
cold.

We all sat along the bench. Tempest perched between me
and his white friend.

"I met Bob down in New Orleans a few weeks ago," Tempest
was saying. "I'd been traveling around for some time and we hit
it off pretty good. Even you'd be surprised by the things he
knows."

"You from Louisiana, Bob?" I asked.

"Not originally, no."

"You know, Angel," Tempest said. "I didn't think I was ever
gonna see your better-than-thou sorry ass again. I was on the
road havin' me a good time. I went through North Carolina and
Atlanta and Miami Beach. Must'a kissed a hundred girls and I
chased every kiss with a shot of bourbon. I almost married this
sloe-eyed girl down in Memphis . . . Marlene was her name.

She was wild and I needed to keep on movin'. She was s'posed t'meet me at the bus station but when she didn't make it, I just climbed on the bus and it rode off."

There was sadness in Tempest's tone but he dropped it almost immediately as he continued.

"I got off the bus in New Orleans and got a job unloading rice off a barge that come down the Mississippi just about every day. I met a white girl named Ellie who loved me almost as much as I did Marlene. She would buy me drinks at night and then take me home to her apartment in the Quarter.

"I had it sweet with that girl. I sure did. But then, on a Wednesday I had off, Ellie went to work and I was layin' up in the house. I started to think about the old days, before I ever met you."

Tempest leveled his gaze at me and I knew that we were about to engage in that seemingly immortal debate over sin and virtue. I began to fear that he would repent and that I would lose my family for eternity.

Tears gathered in my physical eyes. Through the blur I glimpsed Bob—he was smiling at me.

"I was thinking about my mother and my brothers and sisters," Tempest said, "about my wife and children who are also lost to me. I thought about Harlem, sweet Harlem—and I knew that I had to come home.

"I got my things together and headed for the train station—"

"Excuse me," I interrupted.

"Yeah?" Tempest allowed.

"If you were working for a laborer's wage and traveling by bus how could you afford that suit and ring?" I asked. I didn't want to. I didn't want to know that Tempest had committed some crime.

"I was just gettin' there, Angel," Tempest said with a patient smile on his lips. "You see, I stopped at a bar before gettin' to the bus depot. And there I met Bob."

The white man clasped his hands together and nodded.

"Bob," Tempest continued, "is a slick talker and a man with deep insights. He offered to buy me a drink at the bar and before I knew it I was tellin' him my whole life story."

"Everything?" I asked.

"Everything," Tempest said with a shrug.

This should have been impossible. There had been a prohibition implanted in Tempest's brain that would have kept him from telling of his experiences at the pearly gates. The fact that he could resist this spell meant that he had almost broken free from the bonds of heaven.

"Everything," Tempest said again. "And when I was through, Bob here offered to be my lawyer and represent my case to you. He bought my clothes and my plane ticket and came with me up here to Harlem."

My dry tongue and fluttering heart returned. Suddenly I was worried about more than losing my family.

"This is not acceptable," I said with hardly a stammer.

"If Tempest could refuse to accept holy Peter's pronouncement," Bob said, "then it is obvious that you do not issue the rules."

The white man grinned at me, stroking his bare chin as if there were an invisible beard there.

An inkling came into my mind.

"What is your last name, Bob?" I asked. "Or should I say Robert?"

"No," he replied. "Bob is my last name. My first name is rather weak—Basel, after a distant cousin."

"Basel Bob?"

He smiled and my heart went cold.

"Beelzebub," I whispered.

"At your service, accounting angel," he said with a slight bow of his head.

"Tempest," I said. "You are now in league with the devil and still you claim that you are not a sinner?"

"Calm down, Angel," Tempest said. "I ain't in league with nobody. But you can hardly blame me for talkin' to the man."

"He is Satan," I said in a loud and clear baritone.

"But ain't it him you say I belong with?" Tempest asked. "The very reason you here livin' with the woman I love is 'cause you want me to go to hell."

I was silenced by Tempest's claim. Indeed I was sent to earth to convince Tempest that he belonged in hell. And now Satan had sniffed out our weakness. If he could convince Tempest to fully renounce the judgment of heaven then our defenses would be in shambles and even the kingdom might fall.

My role was clear. No petty personal yearnings could stand in the way. The future safety of Branwyn and Tethamalanianti and the past and present generations of earth depended upon the stance I took.

I rose to my feet and spoke in my full celestial voice.

"I will meet your challenge, Satan, and I will argue against your lies. I am on the side of righteousness and you are the worm at the apple's core."

Bob rose and gave a proper bow.

Tempest stood too.

"Cool, dude," Tempest said. "We'll be talkin' to ya."

And they walked off toward Forty-second Street. Almost every pair of eyes in the park were on me, for having heard the full voice of the accounting angel, they were filled with awe and dread.

The Ascendance of Man

S ATAN WORE BLACK hair with a silk T-shirt and slacks to match. There was a ruby ring on the pinky finger of his left hand and reddish brown snakeskin shoes on his feet.

"Joshua," he said, greeting me with my assumed mortal name.

"Bob," I replied in kind.

I was standing at the front door of a brownstone on 159th Street, an address given to me by Tempest Landry by phone that afternoon.

When the call came in I was sitting at my desk thinking about Tempest. But that wasn't unusual, I had been thinking pretty much nonstop about him for the past week, wondering when he and his new friend, the devil, would contact me.

"Come on up to my new pad after work, Angel," he'd said. "Let's get this bad boy on."

BOB BOWED AT THE door and said, "Come in."

I followed him past a stairway to the upper floors into a sumptuous living room. There was jazz playing on a hidden stereo and drinks set out on a glass table that had for its base a silver statue of a naked woman lying on her back.

"Sit," the devil bade me.

I lowered into a stuffed chair covered with real zebra skin.

"Your place?" I asked.

"I'm letting Tempest use it while we're working together. I'm making my home at the new Thai Royale at Union Square. Have you ever stayed there?"

"It's a little beyond my means."

"Oh yes," the beautiful youth said. "Tempest told me. With all the resources of heaven behind him the accounting angel has to work for bookkeepers and live in a six-floor walkup in Staten Island."

"Nothing wrong with honest labor," I replied.

This, I knew, was the beginning of the debate between heaven and hell. Every night for the past eight days I sat up late praying for guidance from my celestial masters, but no counsel came. Here I was, engaged in the most important conflict ever to arise between good and evil—and I was alone, without an ally.

"Work is for suckers," Bob informed me. "There's enough wealth on earth for all men to live with the minimum of effort but instead they sweat and strain going evermore into debt so that people like you and I can pronounce judgment upon them."

"We merely carry out our eternal tasks," I said. "Without us, other gods would arise."

"Hey, boys," a voice interposed.

We turned to see Tempest Landry saunter into the room.

He was dressed in a black and red satin house robe. There were yellow slippers on his dark brown feet.

Satan, in the guise of a white youth, rose to greet his client. He crossed the room and shook the wayward soul's hand. After a moment I stood too.

"Welcome, Tempest," the demon called Bob hailed.

"Hello," I said.

"Damn. You two boys can't hardly wait to get started," Tempest said, coming into the room and sitting on the couch next to his infernal attorney. "I thought this was my case."

"Tempest," I said. "You're making a mistake throwing your lot in with Bob here. He doesn't care about you."

"Listen here, Angel," Tempest said, sitting back on the fur-lined couch. "Ain't nobody I ever met ever cared for me totally—'cept my mother. Ev'rybody I ever met had their own best interests in mind. So what if Bob here got a bone t'pick wit' heaven? All heaven ever did for me was to call me a sinner an' give me a one-way ticket to hell."

"Your sins called for that sentence," I said.

Bob chuckled and laced his perfect fingers around his knee.

"Bob says that he never expected to see me down in his neighborhood," Tempest said. "He told me that a whole bunch'a people come down to him and they haven't done hardly nuthin' wrong."

"You have to consider the source," I said.

"People been sayin' that about me since I was able to talk," Tempest countered.

I realized that our discussion was getting off on the wrong note. My usual way of talking would not work while Tempest had such a powerful partner.

"Okay," I said. "I'm willing to meet you on your own terms. How would you like to proceed?"

My handing over the conditions of our debate made Tempest smile.

"I just wanna be fair, Angel," he said. "You know me coming back down here to Harlem with a new body so that no one from my old life knew me was quite a shock. And then to have you always on my ass tryin' to trip me up so that I have to spend eternity in hell . . . well it's like I don't have any choice whatsoever."

"Which is where I come in," Bob interjected. "I came here to inform this poor soul of his rights. He's the first mortal to at least partially figure out that he has a say in the disposition of his immortal soul. I'm here to make sure that he knows everything."

"'Everything' is a big word," I said.

The devil smiled. "He's afraid of you, did you know that, Tempest?"

"He don't seem scared."

"Ah, but he is," Bob continued. "Haven't you ever wondered why they would send such an important angel as Joshua to come down and try to convince you to accept Peter's rule?"

"He said that my refusal could mess up the accounting practices up there," Tempest said. He was looking into my face.

"That's an understatement," Bob announced. "If you were to renounce Peter's decree all of heaven would be turned on its head. Instead of telling a so-called sinner to go to hell he would have to ask them if they wanted to go. Old cases would be reopened. The boundary between supposed good and evil would be rent asunder and there would be no more separation between his realm and my own."

When Bob looked at me his eyes turned the color of yellow fire opals. His smile was a dagger in my spleen.

"All you have to do is renounce the edict of Peter, and Mr. Angel's soul would be sucked back up into heaven and his wife would be yours for the asking. This sham of an inquisition would be over. And no longer would you be answerable to the shadowy whims of strangers."

If I could have I would have smote Old Nick right there. But he was ruler of hell and I was just a bookkeeper from heaven. He could have banished me from the earth at any time he chose but he did not choose to do so because he wanted to see me suffer. He knew that Tempest would ultimately deny the holy verdict of Peter, that all the faithful aeons of my life would come to nothing and there wasn't a thing I could do to stop it.

"Really?" Tempest asked, as if a child.

"Truly," Bob agreed.

"Let me ask you somethin', Bob," Tempest said. "Do you know of a man named Elrod Jenkins?"

This question was unexpected. The sly demon's brow furrowed. He paused a moment and then said, "No, uh, not off-hand."

"Elrod was somethin'," Tempest said. "He robbed and stole and raped both women and children. Lies flowed from his mouth like water from the Mississippi. And he never respected law or blood or common decency."

"An individual," Bob said, failing to repress a grin.

"You could say that again. I used to see him down at a barber's shop on 133rd. He was a small man and unlikely to overpower many men his own age. But he was devious. They finally got him for the murder of a woman named Bertha Nolde and her three daughters. He robbed 'em and murdered 'em too but he did much worse. Killed the mother last. Now you know that was wrong."

Bob, who had been smiling since he met me at the door, now had a somber countenance.

"You sure you don't know him, Bob?" Tempest asked. "He sound like one'a yours."

"He may well be in my realm," Bob replied. "Peter sends five out of every nine that stand before him to me nowadays."

"That true, Angel?" Tempest asked.

I nodded. What else could I do?

"How about Benny Rogers?" Tempest asked of the devil.

Bob shook his head and grimaced.

"Is he another archfiend?" the devil asked.

"He was Bertha's oldest. He robbed a store and got himself sent to prison with Elrod. They say he stabbed old Elrod a hunnert an' sixty-two times. You know that boy was very dead."

For the first time in many days I grinned. It was now Basel Bob's turn to experience the wily cunning of Tempest Landry.

"Though I don't know either case," Bob said, "I can assure you that Peter will send both men to me."

Tempest turned to me.

"Is that right?" he asked.

"Probably," I said.

"And if I renounce my judgment," he asked Bob, "then Elrod will be loosed on the virgins of heaven?"

"He will be free as you are free," Bob said with almost a stutter on the last word.

"But I ain't no sinner," Tempest said.

"Renounce Peter," Bob commanded, his eyes shining like moons.

"But what would I say to Benny and Bertha when I see'd 'em?" Tempest asked.

"What do you care about them?" Bob replied, floundering in the pedestrian considerations of his client.

"I got to think about this, Bob," Tempest said. "You know you said that you wanted to represent me in my case against Mr. Angel here. But if I got to free Elrod and a dozen more people I know like him, then I don't know if it's right."

"Right?" Bob repeated. He wanted to say more, but words, for the first time in millennia, escaped him.

"Listen, Bob, Angel," Tempest said then. "I got me a girl comin' ovah in a while. Why don't you two leave and I'll call ya when we can continue with this here riddle."

And so Beelzebub and I, Peter's accounting angel, found ourselves on the stoop of Tempest Landry's temporary brownstone abode.

"What just happened?" the devil asked me.

"I don't know, Bob," I said. "Maybe it's the ascendance of man."

Free Will

I WAS WALKING UP the hill to our St. George apartment in Staten Island when a chill went through me. It was raining that November evening and the wind was blowing. My umbrella had been turned inside-out on the way to the ferry. The weather alone could have accounted for the iciness in my bones but still I felt frightened.

I had been living with fear for many days. Each morning I awoke with a sour taste in my mouth after a fitful night threaded with the dread of mortality.

As far back as I could remember (and my memory stretches back to the beginning of time) I had never contemplated an end—but now a single being, Tempest Landry, held the fate of everything I had ever known in his faithless hand. With but a word he could topple the pillars of time.

I shuddered at the top of the hill, walked into our tenement home, and climbed to the sixth floor.

The first thing I saw when I opened the door was Branwyn sitting in a chair. Tethamalanianti, our infant child, was nestled in her arms. I walked in and Branwyn rose, smiling. To my right I saw a man seated on our thin sofa.

"Hey, Angel," Tempest said.

He jumped to his feet and held out a hand.

"Hello," I said, a tentative tremor running through the word.

"Isn't it wonderful, Joshua?" Branwyn said. "Tempest has come back from a long trip and he wants to be friends again."

Branwyn didn't know that I was a true angel nor did she know that Tempest Landry was a wayward soul. She only knew that he had saved her life; that when she fell in love with me he was heartbroken and left his beloved Harlem to get away from the pain.

"It's wonderful," I said, forcing a smile and shaking inside.

Titi made a one-syllable sound and I took her from my lover's arms. The baby's face broke into a smile and for three seconds my love for her took the place of the trepidation in my heart.

"That's a beautiful child you got there, Angel," Tempest said.

He took her from my arms and sat with her on the couch, making goo-goo sounds and letting her grasp his fingers.

Branwyn brought out glasses of red wine and the three of us talked about the days two years before when we all met.

I didn't lie to Branwyn, but neither did I let on that I had known for a few weeks that Tempest was back in New York.

After an hour or so of light banter Branwyn said that she knew we wanted to talk alone. She said that she was going down to our neighbor's apartment to visit for a while.

"Leave the baby," Tempest said.

This request made Branwyn grin from ear to ear.

When she was gone Tempest took the bottle and poured us each a juice glass full.

"That Branwyn is better than the both of us put together," he told me.

"Why are you here, Tempest?"

Tempest had a hardy face with strong features that were like and yet unlike his appearance before his untimely death. None of his friends or family would have recognized him but he was still the same man.

"Why you wanna be rude, man?" he asked. "I just came by to say hey."

"I'm sorry. As you know, I've been under a lot of pressure lately."

Titi giggled in the space between us.

"Yeah, well," Tempest hesitated, "you know that ain't my fault."

"You're the one who decided to throw his lot in with the devil," I reminded him.

"My lot," he said. "That's like where you put up a house, right?"

I took in a deep breath and did not answer.

"I know what you think, Angel," Tempest said. "You think I'm messin' wit' you. You like America."

"What?"

"You think, 'here this little island of a man in league with the devil,' like some little island of a country lookin' to get itself a big bomb."

"What are you talking about, Tempest?" I asked. "You're the one with the power."

"That's what America say," Tempest responded. "We get all

upset when some tiny little country got one bomb even though America gots ten thousand bombs. America say, look at that country over there, they a threat to peace. But what other choice do the little man got, then to get ahold'a what he could an' hope the roof don't fall in?"

"You aren't making any sense, Mr. Landry."

"That's what America say too," Tempest said, raising his voice.

Tethamalanianti turned her head toward him and let out a respondent cry.

"America says," he continued, "that any country that builds for war isn't making any sense. But what choice do they got? Just 'cause you small, just 'cause you poor don't mean that you have to bow down an' take it. I been readin' the papers since I don't have to work every day you know. I sit up in that house Bob give me an' read two, three papers every day. And you better believe I see you an' me on every page."

"I'm not your enemy, Tempest," I said, the thread of truth running through every word.

"That's what I say about myself," Tempest whined plaintively. "When I see all the people dyin' from our bombs and guns and police actions I say, I'm not the enemy of these people.

"But when they get mad at me what can I say? They ask, did your country drop them bombs? And I say yeah, but . . . An' then they ask, did your country kill my eighty-six-year-old grandmother asleep in her bed? And I say, I guess so, but . . . and they ask, is it your soldiers crushin' our thousand-year-old streets with their tanks and threatenin' our young men if they protest and tellin' us who our leaders will be? And all I can say is, but it ain't me."

"What does any of that have to do with our business, Tempest?" I asked.

"I know," Tempest said. "I know what you sayin'. You say that it's free will brought me to your judgment. You say that I did so-and-so and therefore I should accept my punishment. But ain't that exactly what the man with the dead grandmother be tellin' me? Don't he say, 'Tempest, you killed my grand-mother and if ever I get the power I will kill you'? Ain't that what we all afraid of?"

"But you didn't kill his grandmother."

"That's what I'm talkin' about," Tempest said. "I didn't, I know I didn't, but he says that I did. So now I got me a enemy and so I look around for some friends. And who do I see but Bob?"

"But Bob is the greatest evil," I pronounced.

"Maybe that's true," Tempest said. "Maybe he is. But when a man firin' on you with a gun you dive behind the first rock you find. You dive deep. When Bob told me he could solve my problems wit' you I jumped at it. He was the only one offered."

"But you were already free, Tempest. You were traveling and working, kissing girls and drinking whisky. I was no threat to you."

"I hear ya, brother Angel. I was free too. But every mornin' I woke up thinkin' that this might be my last day. Hell was hangin' ovah me and I was scared."

I recognized his fears in my own. I think I grew a little closer to Tempest in that moment.

"But dealing with Satan is wrong," I said. "It doesn't matter how frightened you are."

"That's what America says to the little men and women all ovah the world. We tell 'em that they're wrong to have their leaders and their ways. And then we bomb 'em and bomb 'em again."

"The comparison doesn't work, Tempest. I haven't dropped a bomb on you."

"You would if you could," he said.

I didn't know how to answer so I picked up Titi and kissed her.

"Tell me sumpin', Angel."

"What's that, Tempest?"

"If America was a man would he make it past Peter's threshold? I mean, can a country commit a sin?"

This question stopped me. Many sinners had come up to Peter with the defense, in their hearts, that they were commanded to do terrible things. And in some cases they were forgiven. But more times than not they were sent on to Satan's realm. Better to listen to the gospel than to a mortal leader.

But we had never thought of challenging a nation for its sins. Nations weren't living beings . . . but . . .

"That's what I been thinkin' about, Angel," Tempest said. "The man in charge, the country with the most guns, neither one is ever seen as a sinner. It's only little guys like me get the stick.

"I didn't have no choice but to take Bob's help when he offered it. Either take his help or risk eternity in hell."

"He is hell," I said.

"That's where it gets tricky," Tempest said. "The way I see it, you wanna push me over the cliff and you mad at me that I grabbed on to your leg. It's just like America mad at the little guy for puttin' up a fight before he go down. But I ain't got no choice. I got to grab on. You know it ain't in my nature just to let somebody throw me into a hole. I might have to go but I will fight the whole way down."

"I see that," I said, and I did. "I'm sorry, Tempest. I truly am. But there's nothing I can do to save you."

"Yeah," Tempest said. He stood up. "I guess for a man like me the only livin' he gets is fightin' to stay alive."

He went to the door and pulled it open. Then he looked back at me.

"Tell Brownie that I said she was better than the both of us," he said.

"I will."

PROOF

TEMPEST LANDRY, BEELZEBUB, and I planned to
meet at the Metropolitan Museum of Art for lunch at two
o'clock on a Tuesday afternoon. This meant that I'd have to
make up an excuse to be away from work. My bosses were angry
with me because we were in the middle of an important audit.
The devil wanted me off balance so that I'd slip up in the delicate negotiations between heaven and hell.

Tempest held the key that would either destroy or maintain
the status quo between good and evil. If he were persuaded to
deny heaven's rule, then Satan could, once again, storm our
walls; if Tempest accepted heaven's ruling he would have to
spend eternity in hell.

So far Tempest had not taken sides. He was paid a regular
stipend from Bob and he lived in a brownstone that Bob owned
in Harlem. But Tempest had not yet spurned the Infinite.

It was my hope that he would refrain from either position
because, even though I am an angel, I had fallen in love with a
mortal woman and we had spawned a beautiful child—Tethamalanianti. It was my wish to stay on earth with my family at

least until I was sure that my daughter would have a happy life.

But my wishes were of little concern, compared to the threat Tempest posed to the Infinite.

I stopped at the information desk in the great hall of the museum and asked for directions to the Trustees' Dining Room. The elderly volunteer handed me a small tin badge and said, "Take the elevator to the fourth floor."

"Don't I have to pay?" I asked.

"Your host's membership pays for admission," she informed me.

I PASSED MANY RELIGIOUS icons on the way to the elevator. John the Baptist, Paul, Jesus, even Peter's earthly image was there. All the materials of earth worked, sometimes masterfully, in adoration of the Absolute. As I followed the directions given me by a Pakistani guard I became more confident about my purpose.

"Fourth floor," I said when I entered the elevator.

"Are you a member?" the bespectacled guard asked.

"No."

"Fourth floor is for higher-level members," he informed me.

"I was invited for lunch," I said. "Is there another trustees' dining room?"

"Oh," the pale-faced guard said. "It's okay if a member invited you."

THE REST OF THE museum was crowded with tourists, New Yorkers, and schoolchildren in groups—but the fourth floor was nearly empty.

I turned a corner and saw a singular display case containing a necklace festooned with forty or more five-karat pale green emeralds. It was a fortune just sitting there. A few steps further I came to a podium where two impossibly thin and beautiful women stood. One was white and the other black.

"May I help you?" the black woman asked.

"Mr. Basel Bob," I said.

"Oh yes," she said, dazzling white teeth glinting against her jet-black skin. "Mr. Robert and his other guest are already seated. Follow me."

Since acquiring human form I often found myself distracted by the female form. Walking behind that lovely woman, my thoughts turned to the carnal.

I forced my eyes from her posterior and looked around the room. It was a wide, sunny space with high ceilings and tables that had respectable distances between them. At the far end was a wall comprised wholly of a series of slanted windows that looked over Central Park. There, at the center table, sat my companions.

Bob faced toward the room and Tempest was in a chair that looked out over the park.

Bob stood when the hostess placed my menu next to Tempest.

Tempest turned and smiled.

"We were just talking about you, Josh," the devil said. As usual he wore a black silk T-shirt and black cashmere slacks.

We shook hands and took our seats. I sat down next to Tempest and across from my nemesis.

Out of the window I saw an Egyptian obelisk, at least six thousand years old, standing in the upstart park.

"What were you saying, Bob?"

"Just wondering why you make such a fuss over your inescapable fate."

"What does that mean?" I asked with hardly a flutter.

"Heaven is done," the beautiful youth said. "The world has

changed and so has the notion of the afterlife. With just a word Tempest here could end all your aeons of building. If he doesn't do it, then someone else soon shall."

Bob smiled and brought a hand to his imaginary beard. The ruby on his baby finger gleamed.

He wasn't going to give me a chance to order before forcing the fate of Eternity. This urgency gave me hope.

"What's good here?" I asked.

"The crab cakes," he said with a nod.

Tempest smiled at my composure. I had learned from many months of dealing with him that Tempest liked a man's style above all other attributes.

"We already ordered for you, Angel," the once mortal man said. "I told Bob here that you'd have to get back to work and so your crab cakes are on the way."

"Thanks, Tempest. I appreciate that."

"As I was saying," Satan continued. "Why are you so committed to a sinking ship?"

"I don't understand you," I said. "Heaven stands higher than ever. Its glory has never been greater."

"But for how long?" Bob asked.

"If you have to ask, then the die is not yet cast," I replied.

"It will be when Tempest here refutes your authority," Bob said rather peevishly. "The fate of your pathetic god is in this mere mortal's hands."

"But still, heaven prevails."

"Soon it shall not," Bob whispered. "All Tempest has to do is say the Word."

"But what if he doesn't?" I countered.

"Then someone else will."

"Who?"

"It doesn't matter," Bob said, shrugging.

"When?" I asked.

"Soon."

"Your crab cakes, sir," a waiter said at my shoulder. He put the wide white plate in front of me while two other attendants served Tempest and Bob.

Tempest had a steak done rare, while Bob had a mushroom salad with goat cheese.

"Soon," I said, contemplating the word. "When I was working in the accounting of sins, time had a whole other meaning than it does down here. Sometimes I would ponder a human action for so long, nations could have risen and then fallen into dust. Soon in celestial time can be an eternity for man."

Tempest licked his lips over his steak and turned to me.

"You mean there might not be some soul on Peter's line right now who would also tell him no?" he asked me.

"You could be unique," I said.

"Nonsense," Satan growled, his voice so rough that people from nearby tables glanced and glowered at us.

"I think I might be able to prove it," I said.

"Proof?" Bob raised his hand as if he were going to strike me.

"What proof?" Tempest asked.

I smiled and took a roll from the bread basket. I found great satisfaction in buttering that bread.

"Answer him, worm," the devil ordered me.

I was reminded that success in a conflict like this was likely to raise the hackles of hell. Still, I took a bite of the roll.

"Tempest," I said. "What do you know about your friend Bob here?"

"He payin' me five thousand a week, tax free," the Harlem resident began. "He give me a brownstone and nice clothes and done made my acquaintance with women wouldn't give me a second look in my old life."

Five thousand a week! I had been working at a job for so long that I knew the meaning of that sum.

"Y-yes," I managed to say. "But why, why would he give you all those riches?"

Tempest wasn't slow. The smile on his face spoke of all the intelligence of the human race. He turned to Bob and raised his shoulders.

"The angel got a point," he told his benefactor. "Why buy the apple if you livin' in a orchard?"

Bob did not respond verbally. His eyes turned an opalescent yellow, but there was more than that. My celestial vision gleaned a faint glow emanating from the center of his body. That glow was Satan's rage. I girded myself for the onslaught, being sure that the whole restaurant would soon be engulfed in flames.

But instead it was Basel Bob's turn to smile.

"Excuse me, will you," he said. "I have to go to the toilet."

He stood and strode off past the lovely women and emerald riches.

"Whew!" Tempest wiped three fingers across his brow. "You one brave dude, Angel. Do you know who you was talkin' to?"

"I've known him since men wore mastodon skins and rode on ice floes through the night."

"But you had a army back then. Today all you got now is a penknife and a Timex watch."

The observation tickled me. I began to laugh. It started as just a titter but soon ballooned into a rolling guffaw. Tears flowed from my eyes and my diaphragm ached.

The promise of hell's fury had shaken me to the core and Tempest's apt remark made me acutely aware of my frailty.

Tempest put his hand on my back and asked, "You all right, Angel?"

I sat up and pulled myself together.

It was some while before I could bring myself to speak.

"Thank you, Tempest," I said when I regained composure. "It's nice to know that you're on the side of heaven."

"How many times I got to tell you, Angel?" he said. "I am a black man. I ain't on nobody's side but my own. Devil in white-face on one side, heaven in blackface on the other—that just make me all the more alone."

"Not even you could be that selfish," I said. "Not even you could turn his back on the importance of this conflict."

"You mean the disagreement between heaven and hell?"

"Of course."

"Well you know, Angel, I ain't so high and mighty that I can see from your penthouse view but I know what it's like. I know what it would be if one country gets mad at some other country and they say let's go to war. The men that declare war ain't never gonna carry no guns. They gonna go home to their wife an' kids an' feel sorry for people like me get blowed up while drivin' down the road. They won't even know my name but I still be dead. No, Angel, I am not on your side. You an' Bob wanna kill each other? That's all right wit' me. But don't call me selfish when I slip out the back door an' into the woods."

"Dessert?" the waiter asked us.

He was standing there next to the table; a wide-faced brown-skinned man, from Sri Lanka, maybe.

"I'll just take the cookie plate," the deserter, Tempest, said.

"I'll share his," I said. And then to Tempest, "Should we order for Bob?"

"He won't be back today, Angel," Tempest said. "He got to recover from your proof."

"I am not your enemy, Tempest," I said, a real feeling of camaraderie rising in my chest.

"Yeah. But you ain't no real friend neither."

THE DOOR

IN THE NIGHTMARE I imagined a colossal Tempest Landry towering over heaven's gate, holding the earth above his head with both hands. He was about to shatter both spiritual and phenomenal realms with one act of supreme violence.

"Mercy!" I cried.

I sat up, wild-eyed and sweating in the bed. The sun was not yet risen and Tethamalanianti was sleeping peacefully in her crib.

"What's wrong, baby?" Branwyn asked me.

"Nothing," I said, gasping.

"Was it a bad dream?"

I laughed.

"Was it?" she asked.

"I love you, Branwyn," I told the only woman I had ever known in a physical way.

She smiled and kissed me.

"Is it Tempest?" she wanted to know.

"Why do you say that?"

"Because ever since he been back you been all droopy an' broodin'. Does it have somethin' to do with the business you two was in?"

"Tempest and I do have business," I said. "And maybe that makes me a little nervous."

"Don't you trust him?" Branwyn asked.

"He's a complex man," I allowed. "Sometimes he seems like the best man in the world and at other times he's selfish and even cruel."

"But if you in a jam he will be there for you," Branwyn told me. "He saved my life, you know."

Of course I knew this. When Branwyn had been severely beaten he bought a stolen insurance card and had her in and out of the hospital before anyone was the wiser about the fraud. I had always thought that he had done it to prove something to me about the ways of sin in the mortal realm—but now I had another thought.

"You're right," I said. "You're right."

I got up from bed and started dressing.

"Where you goin'?" Branwyn asked.

"I'm going to talk to Tempest."

"But it's four thirty in the morning."

"It'll be later by the time I get there."

I HURRIED DOWN TO the ferry and got on just as they were closing the doors. I jumped into a cab because I needed to get to him as soon as possible. It was not yet six when the taxi let me off at his address.

I rang the doorbell and knocked for more than five minutes before I heard his voice.

"Who's out there this time'a mornin'?"

"Me."

To my surprise the door came open immediately. Tempest was standing there in white silk pajamas under a red, kimono-like robe.

"Angel," he declared, "am I glad to see you."

He reached out as if he wanted to shake hands but instead he pulled me into the house.

"Man, we got to talk," he told me as we went past the staircase of his brownstone and into the living room.

"I came to tell you something, Tempest," I said.

It was the serious tone in my voice that stopped him. He turned to me and asked, "What's that, Angel?"

"Let's sit down," I said.

I sat on the real zebra-skin chair while Tempest settled on the bear-hide sofa.

"What?" he asked again.

I told him about my dream and about the brief talk I had with Branwyn, leaving out the realization that came to me.

"So what?" he asked. "That was just a dream. Why you had to come all the way up here?"

"You did save Branwyn," I said. "If not for you she would probably be dead now. We would have never gotten together; Tethamalanianti would have never been born."

"Yeah?"

"I have always approached you as a project, Tempest. You were the wayward soul who had to be put back on the proper path."

"Road to hell," he corrected.

"But you also, for whatever reason, are responsible for my happiness."

Tempest scrunched up his face and stared at me through tiny slits. He sat forward and examined me further.

"You're happy here on earth?" he asked. "Here, where you

got to sweat and strain and catch cold and die? You just as happy on a crowded subway car as you was up in heaven?"

"I am more joyful now than ever."

Tempest sat all the way back and brought his hand to the top of his head in amazement.

"So . . . what you tryin' t'tell me?"

"I just wanted to say thank you, Tempest. Your kind heart has touched an immortal soul."

"But you still gonna try and trip me up and send me to hell," he said. "You still gonna try and stop me from pullin' the rug out from under heaven."

"That is my purpose," I said. "I cannot do otherwise. But even though we are engaged in this struggle I have to let you know how grateful I am to you."

"Then why don't you fudge my records an' go back an' tell Peter that there was some kinda mistake? You could get me into heaven an' the devil would be stuck with the short end of the stick."

"If I could, my friend, I would. But we don't lie in heaven. Truth is what makes us strong."

"Damn," Tempest said. "You make it hard on a brother, Angel."

And for a while there we just sat. I yearned to change my nature so that I could do what Tempest desired. I wanted to help him, to save him, but it was he who refused to accept Peter's decree.

"You said that you were happy to see me," I said after a while.

Tempest's head shot up as he remembered.

He stood and said, "Come on wit' me."

There was a door under the staircase that led to the upper floors. This door opened onto a long, slender flight of stairs that led down, down, down. Every twenty steps or so there was a light fixture with a weak bulb that barely illuminated the darkness. We had gone down seventeen hundred and twenty-two steps before getting to the bottom.

The basement was exceptionally small; a compartment no more than twelve feet square with three gray bare walls and one wall that had a dirty yellow door at its center. There were two metal folding chairs that were set in front of the door.

"Sit down, Angel. Let me tell you a story."

We sat side by side and Tempest took in a deep lungful of the dusty air.

"After you told Bob that I might be the only mortal soul to be able to bring down heaven he was mad. I think he was upset because he believed you. He kept talkin' about how you were wrong to think that someone like me could be the Celestial Savior."

"I don't know what he means by that," I said.

"And I know you don't too. Bob told me that heaven would not protect me from him because even if I was this Celestial Savior dude they wouldn't know it. He said that and then he took me down here to this yellah door. He told me that this here was the entrance to hell."

It was just a wooden door. The paint was dingy and cracked, peeling away in places. Through the space between the bottom of the door and the floor I could make out a faint red glow; but this could have just been a red lightbulb on the other side.

"Why did he bring you here?" I asked.

"He told me that one day I would have to open that door—either to go down to eternal damnation or to release all of the tortured souls that hell contains. He said that if I didn't do what he wanted that he would make sure that I suffered for all time."

I had no words of comfort for Tempest. His fate was as terrible as mortal man can experience. There was terror in his eyes and trepidation in his heart but I could not soothe his fears.

"What should I do, man?" Tempest asked. "I mean, it would be better if I just died an' that was that. What good is life forever if it's just torture and pain?"

Again, I had no words.

"Can he do what he say?" Tempest asked.

"Yes."

"He can throw me down into the eternal pit and there's nuthin' you could do?"

"He cannot compel you to go," I said. "But once you've accepted your sins as Peter has detailed them you will pass automatically through that door."

We both turned to look at the peeling yellow portal.

"And even though you know that, you still won't fake my records, like I did with Branwyn's medical insurance card?"

"There are rules, Tempest."

"They got rules down here too, man. If I followed 'em Branwyn be dead, your baby would'a never been born. Who cares about rules when it comes to doin' what's right?"

For aeons I lived in heaven calculating the wages of sin. But in all that time, sifting through immeasurable pain, I never once experienced what it was like to be human and to truly know pain. But here I was being tutored in what suffering meant by a recalcitrant sinner. Tempest's pain touched me, it pressed in from all sides.

"I cannot," I said at last.

"Heaven won't save me even if it means that door opens wide?" he asked.

I shook my head.

Tempest stood up and went to the door. He placed his hand upon the rusted metal knob.

"You know what will happen if I open this here?" he said to me.

I nodded. I didn't have the strength to try and stop him.

His fist tightened on the doorknob.

I muttered, "Good-bye," under my breath. I shut my eyes and lowered my head, expecting the obscenities of hell to explode around me.

But instead I heard Tempest laughing. The sound got louder and louder until I opened my eyes and raised my head.

His back was to me and he was shuddering with the laughter.

Finally he turned, the mirth wide on his face.

"What can you possibly find funny at a time like this?" I asked.

"Do you see me, Angel?"

"Of course I see you."

"Do you really?" he asked, still laughing heartily.

"Yes."

"What do you see?"

"A man wracked with pain and fear," I said. "A man who holds the eschaton, the end of the world in his hands."

"No, baby, that's not it," Tempest said. "I mean, it is partly. I am a man. And do you know how you tell that I am?"

"Tell me."

"Because I'm damned if I do and damned if I don't. That's what a man's life is all about."

He laughed so hard that he doubled over and went down on one knee. I sat, mesmerized by his humor.

Finally, when he regained his footing, we walked back up the seventeen hundred and twenty-two steps to the brownstone. It took quite a while and we had to rest every hundred steps or so.

Tempest chuckled all the way.

After all that exercise Tempest made us scrambled eggs and corncakes. We talked about the weather over the meal and then I was off for work.

SIREN

ON THANKSGIVING, BRANWYN roasted a turkey with bread and chestnut stuffing and prepared fresh cranberries cooked with orange peels. She also made broccoli with a cheddar sauce and a lettuce and blue cheese salad topped with honey-coated walnuts. For dessert there was a rhubarb pie cooling on the windowsill.

While my common-law wife hummed in the kitchen making gravy and sauces for our feast I played on the sofa with Tethamalanianti, our three-month-old daughter. A beautiful brown-skinned child, she lay on her back smiling at me and kicking. Every now and then she'd make a loud chirping noise and raise her hand over her head. This meant that she wanted me to sing.

I have a very deep voice, designed for the celestial choir. I sang her a hymn never heard before on earth. It was a song about the Dream before Creation; an imagined universe that was free from suffering and sin. Titi went silent and stared at me as I sang, the amazement in her eyes reflecting the wonder and love stored in my heart for her.

When I finished the chant I realized that Branwyn was no longer bustling around. I turned toward the kitchen door and saw that she was standing there staring at me adoringly.

Time stopped for a moment. It was a feeling akin to my aeons in heaven. We were full and whole, neither going forward in time nor rehashing the successes and mistakes of the past. It was a moment of grace.

Then there came a knock on the door.

"Our guests," Branwyn said, breaking the trance of our perfect moment.

"What guests?"

"You have to have guests on Thanksgiving, Joshua," she told me. "This is the day we share our bounty."

Before I could protest this intrusion on my perfect life, Branwyn skipped to the door and threw it open.

"Hi, Bell," she sang.

A tall, very dark-skinned woman came in and hugged my lover.

"Hey, honey," she said. "How you doin'?"

"Oh, baby, it couldn't get no bettah if I won the lottery."

The woman Bell gave Branwyn a knowing, and somehow lascivious, look. Then she turned her eyes toward me.

"Is this him?" she asked.

"Joshua Angel, meet Isabel Hargrove."

Isabel was beautiful by any standard. The corners of her eyes slanted upward and her face seemed to contain laughter even when she wasn't smiling.

"That's a good-lookin' man," she said, staring deeply into my eyes.

We stood there—frozen. Again time stopped but this time there was nothing pleasant about the experience. I felt like a live bug being pinned to a corkboard collection of a sadistic child. I wanted to run away or shout out that she should leave.

I might have lost control if Branwyn hadn't come up with Titi in her arms.

"Say hi to Aunt Bell, Titi," Branwyn said.

Bell's eyes ignited with love. She took Titi in her arms and made silly noises that brought peals of glee from my daughter.

They joined me on the couch and chatted about each other, the people they knew and what was happening with them.

Bell was from Montclair, New Jersey. She designed clothes for wealthy clients there. She was living with a man named Stanley but when Branwyn asked how he was doing she said, "I don't know, I don't wanna know, and I don't care either."

There came, at that point, another knock at the door.

I got up to see who it was.

"Hey, Angel," our second guest said.

I can't say that I was surprised to see Tempest Landry, the errant soul, standing there before me.

"Hi, Tempest," Branwyn cried.

"Hey, baby," he said.

They hugged while Bell stared from the sofa.

Branwyn's friend was dressed in tight-fitting black pants and a white silk T-shirt. Her lips were a faint red and her eyes blazed as she stared at Tempest.

Something inside of me began to quiver.

I had been an angel for tens of thousands of years but my time as a corporeal being had been short. I hoped that I had experienced and overcome all of the sinful emotions that arise from physical desire. My actions had been, on the whole, pure. There was the question of what St. Peter would say when he was informed that I had taken an earthly mate and had sired a child by her. But even that impropriety had been done under the spell of love; a word that was the closest thing to currency in heaven.

But the feelings I now experienced were lust and jealousy. I grabbed a chair from our dining table and said, "Here, Tempest—sit."

"Thanks, Angel," my friend said, "but I think I'll sit next to this lonely girl ovah here."

Isabel sat up straight to greet Tempest, the erect posture accenting her figure.

"Bell," she told my mortal charge as she proffered a hand.

"The name is Tempest but you can call me Lover."

The women both laughed. I suppressed the urge to sit down between Tempest and Isabel.

"Now we all here, let's sit down to suppah," Branwyn announced.

Tempest was at his best throughout the meal. He told many a colorful story about the denizens of Harlem. One such tale was about a man who kept a twelve-foot-long pet crocodile in his infirm mother's basement. The man kept his pet alive by flooding the cellar and enticing stray dogs to the basement with handfuls of hamburger meat.

"You know," Tempest said, "crocodile only gotta eat every couple'a weeks and Jimmy was slick about the dogs he took so nobody ever caught on."

"Did he evah get into trouble?" Isabel squealed, laughing at the way in which Tempest spun his tall tale.

"You know he did," Tempest said in such a way as to make the women giggle and my gorge rise.

"How's that?" Isabel asked, touching the sinner's knee.

"A woman. What else?"

"A woman fount his alligator and turnt him in?" Branwyn asked.

"Naw," Tempest said, shaking his head in sorrow. "His girlfriend Sheila was foolin' around with Li'l Willy Parker. You know all the women have a go at Li'l Willy because he was known to be the greatest lover on 152nd Street."

"And why that got him in trouble with that big lizard?" Bell asked.

Tethamalanianti began to cry in my arms. I knew that she was reflecting my growing anger.

"Jimmy told Willy that he got a whole crate of DVD players in his basement and that Li'l Willy could get one of 'em for ten dollars if he met Jimmy at midnight at his house. Li'l Willy came at the stroke'a twelve . . ."

Isabel and Branwyn were enthralled with Tempest.

". . . and Jimmy opened the basement door at the side'a the house," Tempest said. "He told Li'l Willy to go on down. Li'l Willy took two steps on the ladder and that croc jumped all the way outta the water and snapped them big jaws only an inch away from Li'l Willy's face. That boy took off! He said that Jimmy tried to grab him but he was so scared that he could'a knocked ovah Jim Brown and outrun him too."

The ladies were doubled over in laughter.

"The cops come ovah that very morning and arrested Jimmy for assault with the intent to make dinner."

After the laughter had subsided, Tempest turned his attention to me.

"Why you lookin' so glum, Angel? Don't tell me you think that tellin' a good story is a sin?"

"Sin?" Isabel sang. She put her arm around Tempest's shoulders, and my heart sank.

"Oh yeah," Tempest told her. "Me'n Angel been talkin' about sin since the first day we met. Matter'a fact the biggest sinner I ever met have a house up in Harlem. A big ole brownstone."

"Who is that?" Isabel wanted to know.

"Man name'a Bob. He lettin' me stay in his house for a while

so I don't wanna talk him down but he make all the worst crim-
inals you know look like Easter bunnies."

"You live in a brownstone?" Isabel asked.

Tempest nodded.

"How many roommates you got?"

"Just me," he said. "You know I was talkin' to Bob the other
day, Angel."

"Oh?" said I. Tempest was evoking our prime purpose: the
debate over whether or not he was a sinner deserving of hell.
"Yeah," Tempest said. "I asked him what he thought about sin.
He said that all sin was a matter of temptation. He said that if
you put enough temptation in front of somebody they are sure
to succumb sooner or later. I told him that you didn't agree,
that you believed that any mortal could take the high road no
matter how sorely they were tempted."

"Really?" I asked. "And what did he say to that?"

"He said for you to imagine the people you loved most in
the world. Your parents or your children. He said for you to try
and think about what they might do when faced with the choice
between right and wrong. What might a mother do to save her
man or her child?"

This last question I heard in Bob's gruff voice. Fear throttled
me. I couldn't utter a word. I thought of the many conundrums
that Satan could devise to lure Branwyn into committing a mortal crime. I imagined in the years to come the pitfalls he could
put in the way of Titi.

Tempest wasn't grinning as he usually did when he got the
better of me in one of our talks. He loved Branwyn too. His
question was a warning. I am sure that Bob hadn't meant for
him to repeat his threat.

"Tempest," Branwyn said. "You stop messin' wit' my man.
You know that he take all that stuff serious. An' you just be

playin'. So stop. This is Titi's first Thanksgivin' and I will not have you mess it up."

"Okay, baby," Tempest said while he was staring at me. "You the boss here."

"All right," my lover said.

She said more but I wasn't listening. For the first time in all my aeons I felt vulnerable to Beelzebub. He could strike out at me through my loved ones. What could I do to stop him? What would I do?

"Honey?" Branwyn was saying.

"What?"

"Will you sing for us?"

"He could really sing?" Tempest asked.

Isabel had a quizzical look in her eye. She seemed to agree with Tempest. I suppose I didn't look very musical.

I took a deep breath not knowing how it would come out. I exhaled a chant that had not been heard, even in heaven, for more than fifty thousand years. It was a song that the original choir intoned when humans wore animal skins and angels appeared to them as birds and brush fires. It was the Lament of Man; a song that shouted fear in the night and cried out for a voice to succor the mortal singer. And then it became that voice; that deep reassuring voice promising a morning sun and a path without monsters, food for the finding, and a mountain beyond which was a perpetual summer where all the days were warm and where the specter of Death cast no shadow.

I don't know how long the psalm was but when I had finished Branwyn was amazed. Isabel whispered for Tempest to kiss her, which he did. Tethamalanianti was sound asleep.

The sorrow in my heart was exquisite. For the first time I understood my own story.

A Walk in the Park

THAT FIRST WEEK in December it had rained five out of seven days. The temperature hovered in the upper thirties; not quite cold enough for snow or sleet. The sun hadn't been out at all. Tempest left me word to meet with him at a bench under a certain tree at the very center of Central Park. It took me quite a while that Saturday morning to find him but I didn't mind. Branwyn had taken the baby to see her parents in Nyack and so I had the day to pursue my holy avocation: saving heaven from the hands of the most singular mortal, Tempest Landry.

He was wearing brown leather pants and a blue down vest over a long-sleeved black T-shirt. He also wore a black beret, tilted to the side.

"Angel," he said in greeting.

I sat down. Dark clouds hovered to the south, but blue sky shone brightly on the eastern horizon.

"Tempest."

We sat for a while in the chill morning, between better

times and the deluge. Over the past few weeks I had been learning to live with the possibility of annihilation. I was sleeping all night, and often I made it through an entire day without worrying about Tempest evoking his power and putting an end to the rule of heaven.

I sang to my daughter and went through the mindless tasks of preparing tax returns for small businesses across the Tri-State Area. I made love to Branwyn and sometimes watched television shows about people humiliating their God-given bodies and spirits for money.

Nothing made sense on earth, but for some reason I was happier here than I had been in the presence of the secrets of the universe. My life, such as it was, fulfilled me.

"I wanted you to explain to me what a sin is exactly," Tempest said, looking straight in front of him at the black bank of clouds.

"That is a complex question."

"Well let me try an' hone it down for you," he said. "In the Bible it says, Thou shalt not kill."

"Yes," I allowed.

"That was a commandment, right? The top rules from the big man himself."

"Yes."

"Moses brought down those laws, right?"

"He did."

"But Moses killed all kindsa people. Some of 'em innocent children."

"But he was on a mission," I said.

"So he didn't have free will?"

"He did."

"Then he decided to kill the people that he killed, but that was okay."

"Yes," I said again.

"So sometimes there's a rule sayin', Thou shall kill," he suggested.

"That's ridiculous."

"Okay. All right. I'll go along with that. So what about love, Angel?"

"What about it?"

"Is it a sin to love sometimes?"

"No," I said. "Never. Love is a blessing."

"So when Bell left with me last Thanksgivin' and come up to my house in Harlem, that was a blessin'?"

"Did she love you?"

"In every room of that twenty-two-room brownstone."

"I'm not talking about physical love, Tempest."

"Me neither. I mean I guess human beings got to be somewhat physical. I mean if I never saw someone or heard them or felt them, then I wouldn't know that they were there to be loved, right?"

I couldn't think of an argument against Tempest's claim, but I didn't want to agree with him, so I asked, "What are you getting at?"

"I'm sayin' that bein' a human being, I got to have a physical experience to know that I love somebody."

"Love is of the spirit," I said.

"Can Bob love?" Tempest asked, referring to the earthly manifestation of Satan.

"I suppose."

"When he loves, is it a blessing?"

I was stymied by this question and also by the mood Tempest evinced. He was calm and deliberate; unruffled by real or imagined slights dealt him by the world.

"Can you forgive the devil, Angel?" he asked then.

"I have never been asked such a question. The devil does not ask for forgiveness. He plots against the universe."

"So you have to ask to be forgiven?"

"Yes," I said. "How else would you realize your sins?"

"But what if Bob asked you for forgiveness?" Tempest asked. "What if he said to you that he was wrong and could you have pity on him?"

"Again, Tempest, why do you ask?"

"Bell told me that she loved me," he said.

"And how do you feel about her?"

"Her tongue taste like a drink of bottled water," he said.

"That's a physical sensation, not an emotion," I said.

"So are tears," Tempest said, raising his voice. "Tears are just physical but you think they mean something."

"Weeping opens the heart," I explained.

"I used to have this girlfriend, had a husband named Jim. Sometimes when Jim was outta town Tina would call me and I'd come up and keep her company—if you know what I mean."

"I understand."

"Sometimes Jim would get suspicious though and he'd call Tina and say that he knew that she had some man up in his house," Tempest said. "And Tina would get so upset about bein' blamed for bein' untrue that she'd cry all over the phone. One time she short-circuited the thing, it got so wet."

"Her tears were a lie," I told him.

"So her tears was a sin?"

"Yes. Yes."

"I love Bell," he said then. "I cain't get her outta my mind. She live with a man but I still call her house. Sometimes I go all the way out to Montclair and go to a phone booth to call her. If he ain't there, she might come and meet me for a coffee and a quick kiss."

"This sounds like lust, Tempest, not sanctified love."

"But I feel like I love her," he said. "I got love in my heart."

"You are confused."

"So I couldn't know that I was in a sin because I don't think that I am," he said.

"That's why I am here," I told Tempest. "To prove to you that you are a sinner and that you should accept the judgment placed upon you."

"But if I repented could I go to heaven?"

"It's too late for that."

"What if I convinced Bob to repent? What if the devil told you that all he done was wrong, from the apple on down? What would you say to that?"

I felt fear then because I didn't have an answer. Evil never asked for forgiveness—but what if it did? My heavenly masters had not communicated with me since my first days on the mortal plane. What impact would be wrought on eternity with my rejection, or acceptance, of Bob's repentance?

"What's wrong, Angel?" Tempest asked.

I realized that I had gotten to my feet.

"What does your supposed love for Bell, or hers for you, have to do with the atonement of hell?"

"I was thinkin' that if I could bring about peace talks between heaven and hell then maybe me and Bell could have a life down here; have some kids—buy a house in Jersey somewhere."

A fat raindrop fell upon my right hand.

"That is not your place, mortal," I intoned.

"Why not?" Tempest asked. He stood up to face me. "I can talk to you and I can talk to Bob. I can say whatever I want, can't I?"

"It is not your province to forgive," I announced, as if preaching from a mountaintop.

"But what if I was just like a go-between?" he suggested. "I mean, we already know that if Peter don't get me, then Bob surely will. You tellin' me just to lie down an' die without a fight?"

Fat raindrops were falling all around us and on our heads. We stood there unresponsive to the rain.

"You are a sinner, Tempest!" I yelled. "Not a man of peace!"

But that's not what I was feeling. Tempest had opened yet another threat to the balance of eternity. His petty mortal concerns risked unseating all that had ever been. He was a fool and if I had the power I would have reduced his soul to nothingness.

With this thought I became conscious of the strength of my fears. The rain was cascading now. Cold water was down my back and soaking through my underwear. Tempest was drenched too.

I smiled.

He frowned.

"If you are meant for this role," I said, "then so be it."

"I just wanted to tell you, Angel. You know I didn't want it to be no surprise if all of a sudden Bob asked you out to talk."

"Why not, Tempest?" I asked, raising my voice now above the crashing downpour.

"I ain't tryin' t'trick you, man. I'm just out here tryin' to survive."

ON THE SUBWAY RIDE to South Ferry Station I thought about Tempest's words. I knew that they were true; that he had never once in all the time I knew him attempted to fool me. He was just a mortal trying to scramble out from under the weight of heaven.

If that was his destiny, then what was my role?

THE WISH

SOMEBODY HERE TO see you, Mr. Angel," plump Catherine Lawton said from the threshold of my office door.

"Who?"

"He just said to say that his name was Bob."

I'm sure Cathy wondered how a name so plain could cause such terror in me.

I could feel the blood drain from my face and gooseflesh traveling down my arms.

"S-s-send him in," I said.

As always he wore black silk and cashmere, T-shirt and slacks; his white skin in the form of a beautiful young man. The original owner of that body, I was sure, was at this moment writhing in hell.

"Josh," the raspy-voiced youth said with a nod.

He went to one of my walnut guest chairs and sat, spreading out like blight. He swung his left leg up so that it dangled from the arm of the chair, while lolling back staring at me through half-closed lids.

"I thought that we were meeting at five," I said to the nemesis of all that is holy.

"I've come to make a deal with you," he said.

Joy and dread released their pinpricks through body and soul. I felt sure that heaven had already won, or lost, our war with Bob.

"What kind of deal?"

"I want Tempest Landry's soul."

"I don't understand," I said.

"When the devil comes calling there's no question about his intentions," he said, desecrating the form he inhabited with each word.

When I first met Tempest he told me that sin on earth for him was tempered by the racism practiced by white Americans. Hell often works in metaphor, I knew. I wondered, not for the first time, if Beelzebub had chosen his Bob persona as a statement on Tempest's claims. After all, didn't Satan create the temptations and language of sin?

Maybe he was saying, in the way he appeared, that there was some truth to Tempest's claim.

"His soul is not mine to give," I said. "As you know, Peter sentenced Tempest to you but he refused to go. All the power of heaven so far has not been able to coerce him."

"Is this the same heaven that defeated all my armies?" Bob asked in a voice shredded by rage.

"The same." I couldn't repress the smile.

Bob sat up and rubbed his hands together, looking like a hungry fly on a fresh pile of dung.

"He tells me that there might be a détente between your side and mine," he said, making an obscene gesture with those hands.

I actually, audibly, gulped.

Bob laughed agreeably. Then he said, "We have the same goal here, Angel. You want Tempest in hell and so do I. The only question is, how do we do it?"

"You could make him an offer," I suggested.

"Mr. Angel," a man's voice said from the door.

It was Grantman Chin, one of the partners that owned the accounting firm I worked for. He was a tall Asian man, born, I believe, in Beijing. His mother was Japanese and his father Chinese. They lived in Hong Kong but never felt comfortable because their racial union was an unpopular one. This is why they emigrated to America.

"Yes, sir?" I asked the tall, handsome man.

"Are you working on one of our projects?" He was also the watchdog for malingering employees.

Before I could think of an acceptable reply, Bob turned and looked at the tall man.

"Chin," Bob said, pondering. "That name sounds familiar. Do you know a woman named Deirdre Darnell?"

Terror registered on Mr. Chin's face. He took a step backward, stumbled, almost fell, and then fled the vicinity of my office as if it swarmed with angry bees.

Bob turned back to me then, the unhealthy yellow glow still faint in his eyes.

"I want Landry but I can't get a hook into him," Bob said.

"He took your brownstone," I offered.

"Only after I promised that there was no debt involved."

"You've introduced him to some beautiful women, I hear."

"He's in love with a woman named Isabel and she, lamentably, is not one of mine."

"I think he told me," I said, "that you pay him a stipend worth quite a bit to a man in his position . . ."

"You're playing with me, Josh," Lucifer said, a wan smile like a hidden threat stitched upon his lips. "You know that I have tried to use all these tools and more to seduce the nigger."

The word on Satan's breath carried the fever of hatred. His utterance gave me an inkling of the weight that racism might have had on Tempest Landry.

My sympathy must have shown, because Bob smiled. His eyes grew luminescent, filled with that unhealthy yellow.

"Yes," he said. "I have learned to hate Tempest Landry. He seems like an easy mark for damnation. He has lied and coveted and given false testimony. He's stolen from the church, but still when I make him an offer he manages to deny me."

"Why would you expect me to help you?" I asked. "We are enemies."

"You fear Tempest Landry, while I hate him," Bob said reasonably. "You have sentenced him to hell. I would take him if only I knew a way."

"You'd give up the chance to topple the kingdom for a single soul?"

"He will never do my bidding," Bob said.

"But once you've claimed him," I said, "then you could force him to turn against us."

"Once Tempest has passed through to me, his power to reject heaven will be nullified," Satan said.

And as he spoke the words, I knew that he was speaking the truth. Intuition told me I could save Eternity by betraying Tempest.

Bob and I sat there, staring across my desk for a good five minutes. In that time I weighed my responsibilities. Tempest was a threat to the foundation of all that I knew and loved. His damnation would save a thousand generations of human beings. I would have to give up my family and return to my post as Peter's accounting angel, but that was really a small price to pay . . .

"I have one thought," I said.

The devil smiled in anticipation.

TWENTY-FOUR HOURS LATER MY office phone rang.

"Hello?"

"Angel, come meet me at the Starbucks down the street from your office," Tempest said, and then he hung up.

I put on my woolen overcoat and made for the door. As I passed the receptionist's desk Grantman Chin came out to meet me.

"Do you have a site appointment?" he asked.

"Do you remember the man I was speaking to yesterday?" I replied.

The fear was immediate. He jerked his head backward as if I had slapped him.

"It's the man he wanted to get information on," I continued.

Grantman turned away from me and went somewhere in the back.

TEMPEST WAS SITTING AT a small table, drinking from an impossibly large paper cup. His mien was grim. I took a deep breath and sat across from him.

Tempest took a sip from his coffee and glared at me. I, for my part, tried to return the defiant stare. We sat there for a minute and a minute more, and then, at exactly the same moment, we both began laughing.

I leaned back in my chair while Tempest doubled over.

He slapped my knee and I put my hands to the side in a false profession of innocence.

"Man, Angel," Tempest whined. "I never knew you had no sense'a humor. Boy, you pulled the joke of the year right there."

"I was merely trying to help him out," I claimed. "He said

he wanted something to offer you, something that you really wanted."

Tempest tried to say something but he couldn't. All he could manage was another round of laughter.

I got up, ordered a small dark roast, paid for it, and returned to our table to find Tempest still laughing heartily.

"How did you come up with it?" he choked out at last.

"He wanted to know what to offer for your soul," I said.

"And what did you say?"

"I said that the thing you wanted most was to be a white man," I recited. "I said that you wanted to escape from the racism that formed your existence."

Tempest howled. He made so much noise that I feared that they might eject us from the coffeehouse.

When he looked at me I saw that there were tears of mirth in his eyes.

"If you think I'm laughin' now you should'a heard it when Bob made me that offer. I thought it was a joke until I see'd that gold light in his eye. Man, Angel, you know he's mad at you. Damn, I bet ain't nobody made a fool outta him in a thousand years."

"What did he say?"

"He didn't say nuthin'. He just grabbed me by my throat an' nearly choked me to death. I was dyin' but you know it was so funny that I still couldn't stop laughin'. Do I wanna be a white man? Do I wanna be a white man? Damn, Angel, you are truly a funny man."

We sat there for more than half an hour before Tempest calmed down.

We drank in silence for a while until Tempest started talking to me again.

"Bob's mad at me, Angel. He wanna take my soul an' drag it

through the sewer. You know, I wake up in a cold sweat when I think about the things he could do to me."

His sober words dissolved my good cheer.

"What will you do?" I asked.

"I don't know. Maybe, when Bob calms down, I could talk to him about some kinda deal. Maybe I could get him to agree to leave the earth alone."

"He'll never honor an oath," I said.

"But he can be fooled," Tempest countered.

"Yes," I said. "Maybe we could work together and undermine his plans."

"You an' me, Angel," Tempest Landry said.

"You and me," I agreed.

I could almost hear the outraged protests from both heaven and hell.

THE BALANCE

THE NEXT TIME I met Tempest was at a men's social club on 149th Street. It was called the Exeter Club and was no more than a dirty storefront leased by a man named Charles Bigford—who hadn't been seen in over a decade.

When I came in the front door a big woman wearing a wavy red-haired wig stopped me.

"Where you think you goin', sugah?" she asked.

And before I could answer, Tempest shouted from a table against the back wall.

"He's wit' me, Hester."

"Okay," she said with a sneer. "Go on then."

There was a pool table in the center of the room. Two men were playing snooker there. At the three tables against the display window at the front, men were playing dominoes, checkers, and chess.

The place reeked of cigarette smoke and stale beer.

I joined Tempest at his small table. He offered me a cigarette even though he knew I didn't smoke.

"So how did you say this place came into being?" I asked, making small talk before we plotted the fate of the universe.

"Charles won the Lotto some years back," Tempest said. "Eight million dollars' worth. He leased this place so that all of his old friends would have a place to play dominoes and checkers when it was too cold in Morningside Park. He left the deed in the hands of Hester Curly there, and give her a list of the men who were members and who could nominate new members."

"How did you get in?" I asked, knowing that in his new body Tempest had only been on earth a little over two years.

"I give Hester two hunnert dollars from what Bob give me, and she put me on the rolls."

"And what about Mr. Bigford?" I asked my sometime friend and full-time adversary.

"Oh, he don't want nobody to know where he is. You see, Angel, he been a poor man all his life—never lived more than four blocks from where we sittin' right now. He know that all these peoples been his friends and girlfriends, cousins and workmates, would turn against him and either suck him dry or shoot him dead if he stuck around."

"Why would they do that?" I asked.

"Because, Angel," Tempest opined. "People around here don't understand money the way white people and accountants do. For them, their pockets is just a temporary layover for the cash that's workin' its way back into the rich man's vaults. The way they see it if somebody's flush, they should share it. And if they don't, then they're wrong. Kinda like what you would call a sinner. You see, if you ask a poor man what he'd do wit' five million dollars, he'd tell ya that he'd give it to all the people he been around all his life."

"That sounds admirable," I said.

"Yeah. But the minute somebody really strike it rich they

begin to see that what they got ain't as much as it seems. After taxes it shrink down to half, and then with all the family and friends it just about dwindles away. Naw, Charles was right to run. He give his friends a place to drink beer and that's more than they deserve."

With that, Tempest reached into a satchel at his side and came out with a bottle of red wine. He poured me a glass, and then twisted the cap off a bottle of Red Dog beer. We toasted each other and drank deeply.

It was a perfect place to meet. The men in the room made so much noise that our conversation would never be heard, and there was a certain homey comfort amidst the jocularity of the Exeter members.

"How's Branwyn and Titi?" Tempest asked as he refilled my glass.

"Fine. Tethamalanianti can raise her head and sit up now."

"She'll be runnin' the New York marathon before she can say her name," he said. "Where'd you come up with a moniker like that anyways?"

"I named her after a great Mayan princess that lived over twelve hundred years ago," I said. "She was a conundrum in the heavenly court because she killed her father in his sleep."

"Now if that ain't a sin," Tempest said, "then I don't know what is. A child killin' her own father, while he's sleepin' in his bed."

"You would think so," I agreed. "But Autep-Ta had gone mad. On the previous day he had decreed that his four sons were to be slaughtered. You see, he felt that if there was no male heir to take his place that the gods would not let him die."

"Dang. You know a king should be bettah than that. So what happened with Tetha-whatever when she got to Peter?"

"There was much disagreement among the accounting

angels. I was on the side that believed that Tethamalanianti should inherit the kingdom. Finally our side won. She ascended and made a great contribution to our plane."

"Hm. Too bad I didn't have you on my side," Tempest said.

"We are together in our battle against Bob," I offered. "At least we have that."

"How can we beat the devil?" Tempest asked. "He knows every dirty trick in the book. Damn. He wrote the book."

"What if you moved out of his house and got a job and refused his company?" I asked.

"Isabel is partial to our brownstone home," Tempest said. "I wouldn't mind if I had a studio apartment and a dishwashin' job but I don't think I could ever get Bell to leave her boyfriend if that was all I had to offer."

"We're talking about the immortal souls of every man, woman, and child that ever lived," I reminded him, "and who will ever be."

"That's what you talkin' about, Angel. Maybe that's what you see. Me, all I care about is a few creature comforts and a beautiful woman named Bell Hargrove."

"But don't you care about the fate of the world?" I asked.

"People be dyin' by the thousands every day, Angel . . . they dyin' in Sudan an' Congo an' Iraq just t'name three places. But if you go out here in the streets you see people buyin' Christmas trees and video games like they was gonna run out any minute. Nobody care if the world goin' down in flames, just as long as their house don't catch fire."

"But that's wrong."

"Did I make the world?" Tempest asked.

"No. But that doesn't make you innocent."

"If I help you trick the devil an' he go back in his hole will that end the four million dead in Congo?"

"No."

"If you find a way to drive Satan out from Harlem will you get on a plane and try to stop the killin' in Iraq?"

"That's not my job," I said.

"Well if it ain't your job, then how in hell can it be mine?"

"But we've agreed that we should work together," I said, reminding Tempest of our pact.

"I didn't agree to live in poverty so that you could start tryin' to trick me again."

"Okay," I said. "But if you don't forsake the gifts of hell, then how can we convince Bob that he should leave you alone?"

Tempest shook his head.

"Checkmate!" a chess player cried triumphantly.

"What can you do to stop Bob?" Tempest asked.

"I can help you," I said lamely.

"You could tell him that you were going to get me into heaven," Tempest suggested.

"But I cannot. I've already told you that."

"Bob don't know that," Tempest said. "He don't know what you plannin'."

"But that would be a lie."

"What's wrong with lyin' to the devil?"

"I cannot."

"You could tell him that heaven will fight for me."

"But Peter has already sentenced you."

Tempest sat back and shook his head in disgust.

"I swear, Angel. You really can't do a thing."

"I want to help, Tempest. But I just can't think of any power I have to dissuade Bob."

"Why not try and make peace with him?" Tempest said. "Tell him that the fight between good and evil has gone on long enough and that we should have a time of peace."

"There will never be peace between heaven and hell," I said. "That is the eternal struggle. That is why men die, why wars rage, why men must always decide between what is right and what is not."

"And what about me, Angel? What about me? I found a woman I could love and a second chance at life. You got a woman, a baby, a life. What could you give up?"

This question struck very deep in my heart. I knew that once again I was using Tempest for my own ends.

"What if you offered your soul to Bob?" Tempest asked then.

"What?"

"You heard me. For him to spare Branwyn and Titi why don't you give him your soul? I bet you it ain't too often that he gets his hooks into angel flesh."

"Never," I uttered.

"Why not?"

"Because it would be a betrayal of all I hold of value."

"Is your soul better than mine is, Angel?"

"I . . . I . . . I don't know," I said, nearly blinded by the glare of his question.

"Maybe you better go home and figure it out then."

I didn't want to leave. I wanted to say that he didn't understand me, that of course it was he who had to sacrifice. But I didn't know why.

The princess, Tethamalanianti, after killing her father to save her brothers' lives, was sentenced to death by her father's oldest son, who had inherited the crown. She was sacrificed on a stone altar, her blood running in rivulets to four golden cups that the four sons all drank from. My daughter's namesake gave up her own life to save her killers.

"You still here, Angel?" Tempest asked me.

All I could do was stand and walk toward the door.

"Come on back when you ready to talk turkey," he shouted at my back.

The sun had gone down on the streets of Harlem. In the doorways and windows, on the streets and in passing buses there were thousands of people like that noble princess of yore. As I moved among them I felt very small and weak.

ONE VOICE

MANY WEEKS PASSED before I saw Tempest again. This didn't bother me. My life had been filled with small emergencies and pressures. Tethamalanianti, my daughter, had developed a serious skin inflammation and needed a great deal of care. It was tax season and so I was working quite a bit of overtime. My heavenly masters had deserted me as far as I could tell and I had utterly failed in my attempts to lure Tempest away from the influence of Basel Bob.

I awoke at three every morning with Branwyn to ease Titi's suffering by rubbing her with creams. I never got home before ten at night. I worked weekends and spent my time in subways and on the Staten Island Ferry, worrying about hell erupting all over earth and in heaven too.

"You got a fever, baby," Branwyn said on a Thursday morning when I was slow getting out of bed. "You should stay home and rest."

Her eyes surveyed my features and she kissed me. I remember trying to feel love at that moment and failing at that too. It wasn't that I didn't love Branwyn—she was my heart and my life partner—but my inner life was like a battlefield after the war had been fought and lost.

"I have to go," I said. "I've got to get to work."

Branwyn gave me aspirin and orange juice while breast-feeding Titi. I staggered down the stairs, wondering how I could have ever judged humanity without understanding what it meant to suffer.

For a while the aspirin worked on the heat in my blood. But somewhere between the boat and the train the fever returned. Instead of climbing down to the subway I decided to walk over to the Bowling Green Station to take the No. 4 or 5 train uptown.

But on the walk I got lost.

After many long minutes of wandering I found myself on Maiden Lane. The street was crowded with the thousands of people going to work. At one point I looked down and realized that I had lost my briefcase. There were some very important documents in there. I turned to look back down the street I had traveled, looking to see if the attaché case was somewhere. Somebody collided with me from behind and I fell to the ground, hitting my head on the pavement.

It was then that I had the vision.

In heaven there is a place, that's not really a place, called The Field. Here souls gather by the trillions. There, human beings, angels, and rarer beings share music. The resonance of The Field would shatter a planet, the music is so strong. Many times I had gone there to remember what it was that heaven meant.

I went to The Field in my vision but somehow it seemed to me that something was missing; an instrument, maybe even a subordinate aria meant to come in between movements.

"Are you okay, sir?" a young Hispanic man asked me.

"It's flawed," I remember saying.

"Your head is bleeding," he replied. "You should go to a doctor. You want some help?"

"Could one voice be so important?" I replied.

People had gathered around me. A woman gave me a handkerchief and told me to press it against the cut on my head.

I pushed my way out of the circle of kindness and staggered toward the Fulton Street Station. There I found a seat in the last car of the train and fell asleep.

Somehow I awoke at the right stop. As I walked through the crowds the people who saw me drew back in fear but I paid them no mind. I was here to save them, that's what I was thinking.

By the time I got to the front door of the Exeter Club, it was nine forty-seven, and Hester Curly was sitting on her high stool at the door.

"What the hell happened to you, Mr. Angel?" she cried as I entered along with a cold blast of air.

"Tempest here?" I replied.

"In the back room. Through that door there."

The door led to a lopsided hall. The passageway took me to a room that had a refrigerator, a hot plate on a table, and a cot.

Tempest Landry, dressed only in boxer shorts, was sitting on the cot with his head in his hands.

"Hi, Tempest," I said in a voice occluded by phlegm.

As soon as he saw me Tempest jumped to his feet and sat me down on the small bed. He ran from the room and came back with a towel and an ice bucket filled with water. The towel was drenched in red before he was through.

"You burnin' up, Angel," he said to me.

"If I die will I be judged?" I asked him.

"What happened to you?"

"I lost my briefcase."

"Who hit you?" he asked me.

"The ground," I said.

THE NEXT THING I knew I was stretched out on the cot, waking up. Tempest, fully dressed now, was sitting on a backless stool next to the bed, reading a newspaper and shaking his head.

"Hello, Mr. Landry."

"Angel, what's goin' on with you?"

"I heard a symphony without a song," my voice said. I felt far away from the words and the speaker. I was drifting somewhere just beyond reach.

"Go to sleep, man," he said.

"Tell me why."

"Why what?"

"Why."

"Any why?"

I think I must have smiled then because Tempest nodded and went into his tale.

"There was these dudes up in Harlem a few years back," he said. "Called themselves the Brothers even though only two of 'em was even cousins. They was criminal in everything they did. Pimps and burglars, leg-breakers, and even killers if the price was right or somebody crossed one of 'em.

"They all had names but their names don't matter. Not except for two of 'em—a boy named Harley and another one name of James. Harley was the leader and James started seein' his girl on the side. When Harley fount out about it he got the other four and they went out lookin' for James. They caught up with him in a alley under the tracks near 125th Street.

"That same day I was walkin' my son, Hiram Jones, back to

his mother's house—that was my girlfriend Patrice. Hiram was five and he loved the zoo. We had been up there and now we were comin' home in the dark."

Tempest stopped then and looked upward as if to a higher force. My fever was still pretty high and so I cannot be sure of his emotion but there seemed something holy about his demeanor.

"That was just," Tempest continued, "when Harley and his boys caught up to James. They came at him with knives—each one of them taking a turn at cuttin' him until he was on his knees covered in blood. Finally, Harley served him the killin' blow.

"Hiram shouted, 'Look what they doin' to that man, Daddy,' and Harley turned to look at us.

"I was standin' there, Angel, with my boy behind me, ready to throw down and fight those five knife-bearin' men even though I knew I couldn't win.

"Harley stared at me for what felt like forever. Then he pointed at me and then at my boy, and then him and the other four men, whose names I never remember, ran off in the night.

"I went to Patrice's house and told her that she had to make sure that Hiram kept quiet. She moved down to Pittsburgh the very next day. Me, I just sat around for a few weeks thinkin' 'bout what had happened. I wanted to go to the police and tell 'em what I saw. But I knew that Harley an' his 'brothers' would either cut me down or run me out and you know I can't even imagine Harlem without me to be here."

Tempest winced and I fell into a deep sleep.

When I woke up, Isabel Hargrove was sitting where Tempest had been. There were the sounds of men talking wafting in from down the hall.

"Hi, Bell," I croaked.

"Tell me sumpin', Joshua," she said.

"What's that?"

"Tempest says that he cain't get married until you an' him finish some kinda business."

Her face was as lovely as ever. I remember thinking that Branwyn's sometime friend, Bell, was one of the most beautiful women in history.

"Is that what he says?" I asked.

"Yes, it is. And I wanna know what kinda hold it is you got on him."

"Do you love him, Isabel?"

"Yes, I do. Tempest is a good man and you know the Lord ain't let too many of them out the box."

I laughed and then coughed.

"Where's Tempest?" I asked when the fit was over.

"He went to get Branwyn. She comin' t'get you. Now, are you gonna answer me?"

"About our business?"

"Uh-huh."

"No," I said. "I'll never tell."

THE CALL

I T TOOK ME many weeks to recover from the fever I had contracted after walking home in the rain. It was the first real illness I had ever known and my resistance was low to nil. I still went to work, however, because I would have been fired if I took all that time off, and I had a family to support.

I worked all through the tax season at Rendell, Chin, and Mohammed. My days were long, and I went in on weekends too. I lost twenty pounds and walked slowly down to the Staten Island Ferry each morning. I had to leave the apartment fifteen minutes early to make the ferry.

The partners all thanked me for going beyond the call of duty, but they never suggested that I go home early, or take a Saturday off.

This was the first Saturday I got to stay home. I stayed in bed until noon, and then I made it to the sofa in the living room, where I lounged for the rest of the day.

My love, Branwyn, and our infant daughter, Tethamalanianti, kept me company.

"It's so nice to have you home," Branwyn said to me.

"Sometimes you work so much it's like we ain't even got no family."

I used her lap as a pillow while Titi used my cavernous stomach for her bed.

The day passed like a small raft on a calm sea where even the harsh rays of the sun came down lazily.

Tethamalanianti had been making baby talk for a few days. She gabbled on, making another sea, this one of mild baby sounds. I was wrapped in the love of our home.

And so when the phone rang I was shocked that anything could be so loud and jangled. Branwyn stood up, putting my head down further than I wanted it to be. Titi cried to tell us that she didn't want her monologue to be intruded upon.

"Hello?"

In the few seconds that she took to get the caller's identity I dozed off, dreaming about The Song that began the world. It was a song of naming and the first name was the Word . . .

"Josh," Branwyn said. She'd splayed her hand out on my chest and shook me gently. "It's Tempest."

In my torpor on that imagined ocean I heard her words as a warning. A storm is coming, she was saying, a tempest. Then I awoke and handed my cooing daughter into her mother's arms. It took me a full thirty seconds to make it to my feet; another half minute to get to the phone that sat on the ledge of a half wall standing between the living and dining rooms.

I perched on a stool we had there, teetering a bit.

"Hello, Tempest," I said.

"Angel."

It was only a single word, but from it I could tell many things. First was that my earthly charge was under great strain. He spoke my name with a stress on the first syllable that speared my ear. I knew also that he was standing outside. I could hear the roar of traffic and the sounds of people talking, laughing, and calling for taxis. Because of this latter sound I knew that he was in New York, probably midtown. There was also a slight shiver in his voice, so I knew that he was either underdressed or that it was cold outside . . . Physical sensation for me was still a novelty.

"How are you?" I asked my earthly charge.

"I been bettah," he said. "Bob been on my butt like a boil ready to bust."

"How's that?" I asked. I knew that I should have been more concerned, but the exhaustion from the disease left me weak and hollow, void of powerful emotion.

"He come to the house ten days ago and started lecturin' me on the way things got to be. I got to reject you an' Peter, and then praise him and his land beyond the yellah door . . . he said," Tempest continued, "that if I didn't come through for him that he'd crucify my children and put Bell on the slave block; he'd loose disease and famine on the streets of Harlem and castrate me, just for starters.

"I told him to get away from me after the first day. He left, but everywhere I look I see his yellah eyes starin'. If I woke up in the middle of the night I see them shinin' in the corner. If I'm walkin' down the street, babies and grandmothers and cops look like they got them eyes.

"Sometimes I hear him whisperin' in my ear, 'Praise me and th'ow down heaven,' and I get a chill in my heart like I was just about to die."

"An' every night, at midnight exactly, he calls to me."

"You mean he appears to you?" I asked, the fever and its ravages forgotten.

"If I was in his house, yeah," Tempest said. "But I left outta there after the second day. On the third day I was in the Gramercy Park Hotel and he called up to the room."

"What did he say?"

"That he was downstairs, and that I should come to him with his praise on my lips. You bettah believe I didn't get no sleep after that.

"The next night I was sleepin' on a bench in Grand Central Station, when a pay phone started ringin'. It rang and rang and nobody come to answer. That's when I realized that it was just after twelve. I finally picked it up and there he was again. He told me that they were holdin' my berth in his train.

"The next night I was with a lady. We were on the way up to her room when her cell phone rang. She was surprised because she had put it on vibrate but when she answered, it was for me."

"What did he say this time?" I asked, falling into my detail-ridden role of accounting angel.

"I don't know, man. I just disconnected the call and went on about my business with Darla. You know I had enough by then. If that man wanna fool wit' me, then bring it on."

"I don't understand, Tempest. I thought that you were afraid."

"Afraid?" he said into my ear. "Afraid? Man, I passed fear in the train station. I am terrified, petrified, horrified, and scared stiff. You know it was all I could do to hold my own with Darla after that call come through."

"But you actually hung up on Bob. That sounds like a coura-geous, almost fearless act," I said.

"I don't know about all that," he replied. "But I will tell you this—a black man in America, and probably most other places in the world, is most familiar with the county of fear. We spend our whole lives in that particular area of town. We scared'a muggers and policemen, bankers and employers, terrorists and anti-terrorists, meter-readers and little old ladies, fine-lookin'

women and children that look like us just walkin' down the
street. A black man get scared when he cain't think'a nuthin' to
be scared about. So when Bob started this crusade against me
I started to feelin' good."

"Good? You feel good to have your immortal soul under
attack?"

"Yes, sir. That I do."

"I don't understand," I said.

"You should," he told me. "You been on me to admit my so-
called sins and go on down to hell. You act all nice and friendly
but you want me with Bob just as much as he does."

It was true and I did not try to deny or justify my actions.

"I been upset lately, Angel, and I didn't know why, exactly. You
know I been stayin' at the Exeter Club two, three nights a week
and I been gettin' tired of fancy foods and women. That's not me.
I like a big plate'a collard greens, and a woman got some meat to
her. I like Red Dog beer and old clothes when I'm not tryin' to get
with some girl. I thought I wanted all them riches Satan had to
offer, but you know it don't mean much if it don't feed your soul."

"Your soul?" I said, gasping for air from shock and illness.
"Your soul? Tempest, you've never spoken about a soul before."

"I don't talk about goin' to the toilet either, but that don't
mean I don't know about it."

"So why are you calling me?"

"I just want you to know what's goin' on. I just wanted to tell
ya that there's a hellhound on my trail, and who knows what
might become of me. You the only one in the world know my
story, Angel—you and Bob. And even though you'n me don't
really see eye to eye at least you don't try'n muscle me like Bob
is. So if I disappear, or turn up dead, I want you to tell Bell and
the people down at the Exeter what happened. Will you do that
for me, Angel?"

"Of course."

"Thanks, brother. See ya around—if I'm lucky." With that, Tempest hung up.

I sat there, doddering on my stool, thinking that I, a representative of all that claims holiness, had just allowed a mortal soul to go into combat with a great and overwhelming foe.

"What did Tempest have to say, honey?" Branwyn asked.

"Can you lay out my clothes, Brownie?" I answered.

She looked at me and frowned.

"I got to go out there and try to find Tempest," I said. "He's in trouble, and I'm his only friend."

I SPENT THE NEXT four days scouring the streets of Harlem. I couldn't find Tempest, but I hoped that the fact that I was out there looking for him made a difference in the ultimate fate of his soul.

THE
CROSSROADS

TAX SEASON WAS over and things went back to normal at the accounting firm I worked for. I had recovered from the fever that had raged in my system for weeks. My daughter, Tethamalanianti, was crawling around the floors looking for anything that might be of interest to a seven-month-old baby—and Tempest Landry had dropped off the face of the earth.

I had gone to the Harlem brownstone that Satan, aka Basel Bob, had lent to Tempest, but I found the door boarded up and the upper windows obstructed by cinder blocks. I went to the Exeter Club on 149th Street, but Hester Curly told me that she hadn't seen Tempest in many days.

"The last time he was here he had a crazy look in his eye," she told me. "Said that there was a hellhound on his trail."

I filed a missing persons report with the NYPD, but they didn't seem to be worried. They went as far as to check the hospitals and jails. He was not wounded, dead, or incarcerated—officially.

The last time we spoke, Tempest had told me that Bob was hounding him, calling him every night at midnight wherever he was, demanding that he deny heaven and praise hell.

This was Satan's great mistake. The most important aspect of Tempest's character was that he would never give in to a superior force—not even under the threat of eternal damnation. When faced with the judgment of heaven, Tempest refused to bow down. His was the first mortal soul of all time to refuse our damnation.

I say "our" because I was the head accounting angel standing for millennia at the side of whatever saint it was that decreed the fate of the souls of dead men.

NOW MY MISSION SEEMED moot. Tempest had most probably been slaughtered by one of Bob's minions. I knew from the demon's own lips that he had come to hate Tempest and there was at least one time where Satan tried to strangle my nemesis and friend.

The days felt empty. Heaven made no contact with me. Tempest and Bob were both gone. I still loved Branwyn, my mate, and Titi, our daughter. But I had no mission. Days began to fade into one another and familial love was not enough to buoy me.

And then, on a Monday afternoon, when I left out of my office, I saw a man sitting on a bench, eating an apple.

"Tempest!"

He looked up at me and smiled. Then he took a big bite out of the oversized red apple.

I rushed across the street, afraid that he might disappear, as had been the case in the dreams I had almost every night. He reached out a hand and I grabbed him by the wrist, dragged him to his feet, and threw my arms around him in abandon and in tears.

"You're alive."

He pushed me away saying, "That's all right, Angel. You don't have to get all mushy an' stuff. I'm here."

"What happened?" I asked.

"Sit yourself down, Joshua," he said, "and I will tell you a tale."

I saw that he had a bag of red apples sitting next to him on the bench.

"You plan to eat all those?" I asked.

"Them an' more," he said. "Them an' more."

"What happened with Bob?"

Tempest was a good-looking man; brownish-black, in his mid-thirties, sharp in his appearance but at the same time rather kind around the eyes. Women loved him and men wanted to be his friend. He was a fair storyteller and not above playing with the actual facts as he knew them.

"You know Bob wanted me in the worst way," he began. "Said he had a hunger that only my soul would satisfy. I was sweatin' molten steel there for a while."

Tempest shook his head and took another bite from his apple.

"And . . ." I coaxed.

"And then it dawned on me."

Tempest's smile was a thing to behold. It was a very human expression—not weak exactly but biased, not catholic as all expressions in heaven tend to be.

"The morning sun?" I asked.

"It always amazes me when you show a sense'a humor, Angel. When I first met you, you was always so serious about right and wrong."

"I still am," I protested.

"Yeah, but you seen enough down here to know that bein' right ain't always that easy. I mean sometimes you got shades of black you be dealin' with."

"Tempest."

"What?"

"What dawned upon you?"

"Bob did."

"And how did he do that?"

"Well you know how I told you that he be on me day and night?"

"Yes."

"An' how he says he want me to reject heaven and call him my lord?"

"Yes."

"Well that was the answer."

"What?"

"I had to wonder why he be pushin' on me so hard? I mean there wasn't no rush. There been a heaven and a hell since before the church, since before there was a China or ancient Nubia or Kush."

"How do you know about those places?" I asked, distracted by his historical expertise.

"All that downtime I had while Bob was payin' my bills, I got to study," he replied.

"You were reading history in the devil's house?"

"TV," he said. "Sometimes, when I was waitin' on Judge Judy I'd turn to PBS. They had a whole five weeks on the ancient world. And I was thinkin' that all them ancient nations had a God and a devil too."

I nodded, realizing that Tempest was going to stretch out his story as far as it would go.

"So why was Bob in such a hurry?" I asked.

A calmness had settled over me. The reappearance of Tempest reassured me somehow. I had come to look forward to our meandering debates over good and evil. There was a rightness to the feeling I had when we argued.

"Bob was worried because the same power I had over you I also had over him."

An arctic chill set in on me then.

"What have you done?" I asked him. "What have you done?"

Without my willing it so, I had risen to my feet. My celestial baritone filled the streets around us. People turned to stare at us all up and down the block.

Tempest was still seated on the bench, smiling up at me. He took another apple from his sack and took a bite.

"Sit down, Angel. I ain't even told you what I figured out yet."

A palsy entered my limbs and I shivered so badly that if I had not sat down I would have fallen. My teeth chattered and my fingers trembled. I could feel my heart throbbing and a bass drum pounding in my head.

"Bob wanted me to overthrow heaven so that I didn't do the same thing to hell," Tempest said.

He sounded as if he were very far away. My sense of perspective was out of whack, and without a sensible viewpoint my balance went askew. I had to grab on to the stone bench so that I didn't slide off onto the sidewalk.

"I figured that all I had to do," the confirmed Harlemite continued, "was to tell Bob that I didn't accept the rule of hell and his home would crumble just like it would if I did that with heaven.

"I told Bob what I thought and even his white skin went pale. He falled down on his knees and begged me not to do it. He said that hell was filled with people who would cease to exist if I were to deny his validity.

"I didn't see where keepin' people alive and sufferin' was a better choice. But Bob said that hell was like earth in many ways; that people lived there too. Sometimes they suffered and sometimes not.

"Then he said that many souls could work themselves free one day and enjoy the fruits of heaven. Is that so, Angel?"

"Y-yes," I stammered.

"I thought so. And you know I didn't want to get into some situation where I messed up the lives of so many souls. So right there on the crossroads of Frederick Douglass and 125th Street, at midnight, I made my deal with the devil."

"What was that?" I heard myself asking, afraid that heaven had already been demolished while I dithered away my time on earth.

"I told him that as long as he left me alone that I'd leave him alone. I said that hell was safe from me as long as I was safe from him."

"And what did he say?"

"He said, 'Deal,' and shook my hand. Then he turned his back and walked away. I swear he disappeared in the crowd just like a shadow in the night."

"So Bob is gone?"

"Back in the pit with the heads of the different political parties."

"You made a deal with the devil without selling your soul," I said. "Congratulations. That is another first."

"Will heaven make me the same deal?" Tempest asked.

He took a bite out of his apple with gusto and a grin.

I stared at him, wondering if he was part of some greater celestial plan that was beyond my poor reckoning.

"No," I said. "We will not deal with a sinner. You are Lucifer's subject and shall ever be in our eyes."

"But I still don't have to go there unless you can convince me that I'm a sinner."

"I will one day succeed in that task," I warned.

"You want a apple?" he replied.

VISITING
PRIVILEGES

I SAT AT THE far end of a long row of visitors' chairs set on one side of a bulletproof glass divider. It wasn't a very busy day and so there was a seat separating almost every visitor. There were old women and young, a few well-dressed men, mostly lawyers I guessed, and for each visitor there was a convict dressed in gray, leaning forward with a telephone receiver pressed to his head.

There were maybe a dozen felons conversing through the intercom system and just as many guards in blue uniform standing a few feet away. Behind the row of guards was a bright red door with yellow letters stenciled on it: PRISONERS: DO NOT TOUCH.

The door opened and Tempest Landry, aka Ezzard Walcott, walked in with his hands and feet manacled, followed by two guards. The burly guards, one white and the other black, led Tempest to the chair in front of me and pushed him down.

Up close, through the three-inch glass, I could see that there were bruises and a few cuts and developing scars on my ward's face. He stared at me through the glass, making no attempt at first to reach for the receiver. His visage wasn't exactly what I would have called hardened. There was pain in his eyes, determination in the set of his jaw, and condemnation (even hatred) in the long moment of silence.

I reached for the visitor's phone and pressed it to my ear. Tempest's nostrils flared and then he, reaching out with both hands, did the same.

"What happened to your face?" I asked him.

After another sixty seconds of silence he said, "Same thing that happened to my ribs and back, my gut, and the back of my head."

"Who did this to you?"

"Who didn't?"

"What happened, Tempest?"

He almost hung up his phone then. I could see the rage he felt at my show of sympathy. And I couldn't blame him. It wasn't his fault that he was in jail.

"What happened?" he said. "You mean between me and the man who wanted to rob me of my one pack of cigarettes or the two men who wanted me to make them both happy at the same time? You talkin' 'bout the guard I talked back to or the fool I had to slash his face?"

"You stabbed someone?"

"Slashed him," Tempest corrected. "Big dude sayin' I was his bitch any time he wanted. Either I was gonna show that wasn't true or every day would be Valentine's Day for the next eighteen years."

"I'm sorry."

"Don't say that again, Angel. Don't say it, man. You say it and we ain't nevah gonna talk again. You understand me?"

"Yes."

"Good. Good. Now you explain to me why I'm here. Explain

to me why I got Ezzard Walcott's fingerprints. Explain to me why the hell the cops could pick me up and put me in prison without so much as a trial."

"Mr. Walcott had been convicted of aggravated assault," I said. "That and second-degree manslaughter and, and while he was on the run he received more time for flight from justice."

"I know all that," Tempest said, managing not to shout. "I know all that. Question is why am I in his body?"

"Mr. Walcott, after he fled bail, went to stay with a girlfriend—Fredda Lane. She secreted him in the basement of her stepfather's house. It was winter and he was down in Florida staying with his daughter."

"I don't need no weather report, Angel. What I wanna know is what all this gotta do wit' me."

"Fredda's cousin, Dominique, brought Ezzard some food one day when Fredda was with her mother. One thing led to another and Fredda found out. Something to do with an item of clothing. I'm not sure because it wasn't my case."

"Just go on, man," Tempest said peevishly.

"Calm down," the black guard said.

"Fredda got Ezzard drunk and then lured him on the back of a late-night Staten Island Ferry. She pushed him over the side into wintry waters."

"And that's the body you an' Peter decided to put me into?" Tempest asked.

"The whole story wasn't known at the time of your, your transmigration."

"You mean you got all the resources of heaven at your beck and call and all you could do was put my soul in the body of a wanted man?"

"It is regrettable," I said.

"Okay, all right. I'll forgive you but first wave your wings or sumpin' an' get me the heck outta here."

It was my turn to be silent. I wanted to speak but there were no words I had that he wanted to hear.

"What's wrong, Angel? I know you not gonna blame me for what Ezzard Walcott done done."

"No . . . of course not."

"Come on, Angel. I already been in here three months. You know there ain't no justice in that."

"No."

"Well then wrinkle your nose or say alakazam or sumpin'. Just make this here right."

"I only found out yesterday that you were here, Tempest," I said. "I was sitting with baby daughter on the sofa when Gabriel appeared to me. He said that heaven was not pleased with my common-law marriage or my fathering little Tethamalanianti. I have been stripped of my post as head accounting angel and ordered to make you accept the edict of the On High."

"Make me? What happened to free will?"

"They are afraid of you, Tempest."

"Did you tell 'em that I met Satan and defeated him?"

"That disturbed the Celestial Choir even more. The fact that you met with Basel Bob, Beelzebub, further convinced them that you need to be thrown down into Hades."

"But Bob told me that I could tear down the walls of heaven if I just refused to accept your authority. All I got to do is say no to our talks and the whole history of Man and God will come to an end."

It was true. The hegemony of the divine hung by a slender thread, dependent on the whim of Tempest Landry's errant soul. After being shot down dead in the streets of Harlem he refused to accept his sentence into hell. His free will threatened all that has ever been known as true.

"Ain't that right, Angel?"

After a very long time I nodded and whispered, "Yes."

"Then let me outta here 'fore I put an end to you and your whole damn line!"

"I said keep it down," the black guard growled. "One more time an' you back in solitary."

Tempest and I stared into each other's eyes with deep concentration.

"Well?" he asked me.

"I haven't the power to release you, Tempest. I told Gabriel that you might end everything with a word but he told me to meet with you until you broke . . . until you accepted heaven's edict and trundled down to hell."

"You know what Bob said he would do to me if I went down there. He'd torture me with 'is own hands, break every bone in my body just for starters."

"Yes."

"So you ain't leavin' me no choice."

"Men always have a choice," I said in a celestial timbre. People on both sides of the glass glanced in my direction before going back to their conversations and jobs.

"That boomin' voice don't change things, Angel. I'm still up here in prison no mattah what you say."

Again I fell silent. Tempest was the only friend I'd ever had throughout the millennia. He introduced me to my wife, taught me more about life than I had ever learned counting sins and helping to damn offenders. I didn't want him in that prison but I was as helpless as he was.

"So what's your answer?" he asked me.

"I do not have the power to free you. I have been stripped of every benefit of heaven. If I were you I would . . . I would deny the fearful cold winds that envelop you."

"So you agree?" he asked. "You believe that I should tear down the walls of heaven?"

"Gabriel gave me a message for you," I said, reluctantly.

"What's that?"

"He told me to tell you that the demolition of the Divine would not ameliorate your plight, that you would spend the rest of your life in prison and then be thrown into the Abyss thereafter.

"I know you told me not to say it but I'm sorry, Tempest. I have no control over these events. I'm a tool in this struggle, as much a victim as are you."

"Time's up," the white guard said.

They grabbed Tempest by his armpits and lifted him to his feet. The phone fell from his hand but he did not stop staring at me. He craned his neck to keep me in sight as they dragged him away.

I sat in that hard metal visitor's chair for many long minutes trying to figure out what had happened and how I felt about it.

When no answer came I got to my feet and staggered out of the prison: a pawn in a war that I barely understood, a lost soul who had forgotten his destination home.